Robert Bell

Mothers and Daughters

A Comedy in Five Acts as Performed Once

Robert Bell

Mothers and Daughters
A Comedy in Five Acts as Performed Once

ISBN/EAN: 9783743393776

Manufactured in Europe, USA, Canada, Australia, Japa

Cover: Foto ©Andreas Hilbeck / pixelio.de

Manufactured and distributed by brebook publishing software (www.brebook.com)

Robert Bell

Mothers and Daughters

MOTHERS AND DAUGHTERS:

A Comedy,

IN FIVE ACTS.

AS PERFORMED

ONCE

(THOUGH "ANNOUNCED FOR REPETITION AMIDST CONSIDERABLE
APPLAUSE"—*Times.*)

AT

THE THEATRE ROYAL, COVENT GARDEN,

ON THE 24TH JANUARY, 1843.

BY ROBERT BELL, Esq.

AUTHOR OF "MARRIAGE," &c.

SECOND EDITION;

WITH AN EXPLANATORY PREFACE.

LONDON:

JOHN MORTIMER, ADELAIDE STREET,
TRAFALGAR SQUARE.

MDCCCXLIV.

C. WHITING, BEAUFORT HOUSE, STRAND.

CHARACTERS IN THE COMEDY.

LADY MANIFOLD.

EMILY MANIFOLD.

MABEL TREVOR.

ROSE.

LORD MERLIN.

MR. SANDFORD.

LOOP.

CUSHION.

SIR GREGORY PLUMP.

CAPT. SWINFORD HASTINGS,

  MONTAGUE.

BLUNT.   TOM.

Represented at Covent Garden Theatre on the 24th January, 1843, by the following ladies and gentlemen :

MRS. ORGER.

MRS. WALTER LACY.

MISS VANDENHOFF.

MRS. HUMBY.

MR. VANDENHOFF.

MR. COOPER.

MR. WIGAN.

MR. GRANBY.

MR. BARTLEY.

MR. HARLEY.

MR. MEADOWS.

MR. J. RIDGWAY.

TO WHOM,

AS A MARK OF HIS GRATEFUL SENSE OF THEIR
EXERTIONS ON THAT OCCASION,

AND

OF HIS REGRET THAT THEIR EXERTIONS SHOULD HAVE
BEEN MADE IN VAIN,

THE AUTHOR

BEGS TO INSCRIBE

THIS COMEDY.

b 2

PREFACE.

THE drama is a lottery, in which the blanks have a woful preponderance. Worse still—one may gain a prize in this lottery at a heavy loss.

The fortunes of plays are as various as their plots, with this additional perplexity, peculiarly their own—that tragedies occasionally end in laughter, and comedies sometimes come to a tragical close. " The Rivals" was hissed off the stage. " The Iron Chest," failing through the opium of Kemble, was carried triumphantly by the mercury of Elliston. The Duke of Buckingham crushed a play of Dryden's by a witticism ; and the most finished of Congreve's comedies was hardly endured on the first night. But these are vulgar vicissitudes. All such disasters fall within the compass of ordinary probabilities. The fate of " Mothers and Daughters " is unique. It is a case *per se.* Nothing like it ever happened before, and I hope nothing like it may ever happen again. And it is solely in the desire to prevent it from passing into a precedent, that the adventures of this comedy are herein about to be narrated.

Some plays have been enthusiastically received by managers, and then turned out of doors by audiences. But here is a play which was enthusiastically received by the audience, and then turned out of doors by the manager. Some plays have unfortunately failed; but here is a play which succeeded unfortunately. Managers are generally glad to cultivate the prospect of profit held out by a successful novelty; but here is a case in which the manager took considerable pains to prevent the successful novelty from becoming profitable to himself or any body else. This last statement, in a commercial country like England, (and, of course, it is only in a commercial point of view I have any right to suppose it can affect the manager's credit) will be entirely unintelligible. But I beg the courteous reader to bear in mind that I do not expect him to understand it. I do not understand it myself, and am never likely to be able to understand it, though I have left no means or methods of investigation untried—no avenues of enquiry unexplored—no oracles unquestioned— to obtain a satisfactory explanation of the reason why Mr. Bunn treated, not me so ill, but himself. There are some things, however, not the less true, merely because they are incredible.

When this piece was written, it was sent to Mr. Webster, to whom the fugitive Comic Muse of these latter times has always appealed with confidence; and I have never heard of an instance in which she appealed in vain. His reception of the play was frank and cordial; and his opinion of it more flattering than it would become me to repeat. But even managers themselves cannot always control the adverse destinies of plays. Mr. Webster thought the principal character peculiarly adapted for Mr. Farren. I thought so too. He is a wise man who does not occasionally reckon without his host. Mr. Farren thought differently. He might have been right—although there is a proverb which hints that people are not always the best judges in their own cases. But, right or wrong, his opinion on the point was final. There was nobody else who *could* play the character—at least, while Mr. Farren was in the theatre. It was *aut Cæsar aut nihil.* I did not put Mr. Webster to the pain of deciding the question for me; for I felt that it would be a pain to him, and that it would be ungracious in me to inflict it upon him. I withdrew the comedy from the Haymarket.

But I cannot change the scene to St. James's Place, where the comedy shortly afterwards found itself, one bright sunny morning, in the hands of Mr. Bunn, without taking this opportunity of expressing my earnest sense of the courtesy and kindness I have received from Mr. Webster. I am the more anxious to do this, because I believe the charge against managers is generally well-founded, of a want of candour and sympathy and *bienséance;*—(a want, by the way, for which some very extenuating circumstances might be reasonably pleaded in the difficulties and responsibilities of a position, often harassing and invidious, and for which dramatists do not always make sufficient allowance)—and because I believe no manager, at any period, has ever been less obnoxious to imputations of that sort than Mr. Webster. At least so much is due from me personally; and I gladly render this tribute to the public merits of a gentleman who has certainly done more than anybody else for the encouragement of English comedy.

Well—the next scene in this eventful history was St. James's Place. Mr. Bunn had just entered upon the management of Covent Garden. It was the only theatre at which this comedy could then be produced; and the only alternative that seemed open to me, was either to put the MS. into the fire, or into the hands of Mr. Bunn. I decided upon the latter course. Perhaps I ought to have preferred the former; but MSS. are so slow in their growth, that while they are growing to maturity, one is apt to acquire a foolish habit of hoping a better fate for them. Mr. Bunn's approval of the play was no less emphatic than Mr. Webster's. I had the managers with me at all events, and it seemed as if Fortune could never weary of doing me good offices in every direction, except that which led to the critical sanction of Mr. Farren.

Strangely enough, Mr. Bunn had no sooner read the comedy, than he arrived at the conclusion that Mr. Farren was the only actor who could do justice to the character of *Lord Merlin;* and, before he had communicated with me on the subject, he actually offered him an engagement for the two months of the Haymarket recess, to appear in this very part! Mr. Bunn was, of course, ignorant of Mr. Farren's judgment in the matter. But in any case Mr. Farren could not come. He had provincial engagements.

It is worthy of note, that both managers, men of experience and observation, thought the character peculiarly suited to Mr. Farren; but that Mr. Farren, to use the green-room phrase, could not see himself in it. If actors were never to play parts, except such parts as they could see themselves in beforehand, they would do themselves great injustice. True genius must create as well as embody.

Mr. Bunn confessed frankly to me that he felt the want of Mr. Farren in this part, a terrible difficulty. But as there are different aspects to the same humanity, and different modes of presenting and yet preserving the same truth, I did not think it an insuperable difficulty. I thought it possible that a comedy might be played without Mr. Farren; by which I hope nobody will suppose that I undervalue Mr. Farren's conspicuous abilities. I merely drew that inference from the fact that comedies had been produced on the English stage before Mr. Farren's time, and from the presumption that they might continue to be produced even in time to come. I thought that, as there was a serious side to the character of *Lord Merlin*, as well as a comic one, and as, indeed, there lay a very grave purpose at the bottom, an actor of a totally opposite cast might bring out the expression of the portrait as justly, although, perhaps, not so effectively, as Mr. Farren. I ventured to suggest this to Mr. Bunn.

The comedy was now handed over to the stage-manager. It was a step nearer to the green-room. It had arrived in the theatre, and been read by Mr. Bartley—upon whose judgment I place especial stress—who literally pronounced a panegyric upon it. Certainly there never was a play had so many cheering and unexceptionable and influential omens in its favour. Had I been skilled in astrology, I might have begun to suspect that my lucky star was shining *too* brightly.

Mr. Bartley had but one misgiving. What was to be done with *Lord Merlin?* There was but one individual on the stage who could realize the author's precise intention ; and that individual was Mr. Farren ! Mr. Bartley's impression on this point was so strong, that he could hardly credit the fact that Mr. Farren held a different opinion ; he seemed to think that it was like Mr. Farren differing from Mr. Farren. But so it was ; and there was no help for it. It was suggested that Mr. Vandenhoff should be requested to read the part. This was, if you please, a leap in the dark. The character was out of his usual way. But I have great faith in what may be done by a man of superior attainments when he applies himself to a new pursuit. I was not disappointed in the sequel ; and if the comedy had not been strangled in its cradle, Mr. Vandenhoff would have ably vindicated the propriety of an experiment which I cannot sufficiently thank him for having undertaken.

In the meanwhile Mr. Bartley expressed considerable hesitation about the cast generally. He was obliging enough to say that the comedy required a much stronger cast than the resources of the theatre could command : that it wanted such actors as Elliston, Munden, and others of that day ; and, with a friendly zeal for which I am bound to be grateful, he advised me to reconsider the prudence of bringing it out under such circumstances. He assured me that instead of running thirty or forty nights, as, properly cast, it ought to run, it would probably not live beyond fifteen or twenty.* I refer to Mr. Bartley's

---

" If the comedy were mine," was one of Mr. Bartley's observations, " I should lock it up like a bank-post bill, and wait patiently." " So should I," was the answer, " *if you could tell me when it would be due.*" The whole affair is a practical commentary on the present state of our theatres. A dramatist gets a play enacted, not when he ought, but when he can.

judicious counsel, because it is due to him to acknowledge
the soundness of his advice; and also for the sake of showing that I voluntarily incurred the risk of running only
fifteen or twenty nights, presuming the comedy to succeed
on the first night, which was the great risk after all.

Mr. Vandenhoff had now read the comedy, and was of
opinion that he *could* make something of *Lord Merlin*. He
felt, of course, that it was rather a novel attempt for a tragedian ; but that was not his chief embarrassment. The
truth was, that the whole time he was reading and studying
the part, he could not help feeling as if there was an en-
chantment over the words ; as if there was a Mephisto-
philes in the shape of Mr. Farren at his elbow, repeating
them in his ear; and, for the life of him—of Mr. Vandenhoff, the tragedian—he could not help instinctively imitat-
ing Mr. Farren in his own mind, as he read the part, line
by line. In short, he would have felt no difficulty in playing *Lord Merlin* as Mr. Farren, but was, for that very
reason, somewhat puzzled how to play it as Mr. Vandenhoff. Alas! every body could see Mr. Farren in it, except
Mr. Farren himself!

It was a heavy trouble to me that, whichever way I
turned, this image of Mr. Farren rose up before me, with
that jaunty, pinched, old-gentlemanly air, so familiar to the
public, and which seemed in every body's imagination the
exact ideal of *Lord Merlin*. Even Mr. Vandenhoff at
rehearsal looked as if he had been bewitched into a sort
of wraith of the absent comedian;—and people cracked
spectral jokes about him, which had something of the
ghastly effect of blue lights let in upon a scene of high comedy. Nothing could be more humorously dismal. The
figure haunted me incessantly, and its sharp, licorous tones

every now and then seemed to ring through the dialogue. There was no getting rid of it. I tried all sorts of exorcisms in vain. The Presence, like an ill-omened bird, brooded over the play to the last. All this was well enough, or ill enough, through the twilight rehearsals, on the dim, shadowy stage at noon, when, whatever scanty light there was could only straggle in obliquely through strange loops in the roof; but it was to be hoped that this night-mare, or day-mare, would vanish in the broad lustre of the lighted theatre, when the heart of the merry audience would be stirred by eager expectation, and the Action to be realized, whatever might be the issue, would at least have the advantage of being developed in Shapes too palpable to admit of any disturbing influences. I thought I was safe here at all events, and that Mr. Vandenhoff's *Lord Merlin* would be a portrait so individual and distinct, and, above all, so unlike Mr. Farren, that nobody could trace in it—or in the character as rendered by Mr. Vandenhoff—any of Mr. Farren's peculiar and dissimilar lineaments. I was mistaken. Like the grisly head of Winter in the Painted Hall at Greenwich, the eyes of Mr. Farren glared upon me through *Lord Merlin*, move where I would; and as invisible ink gives out precisely the same purport, no matter by whose hand it is held to the fire, so *Lord Merlin* was still Mr. Farren, let who would assume the costume and " speak the speech." The critics unanimously declared that they saw Mr. Farren all through the part. Their unanimity on this point was so remarkable, that one might almost suspect it to have been got up by concert or stratagem.*

---

* " We should presume that this comedy was intended for the Haymarket, and that Mr. Bell took measure of Mr. W. Farren for the part of Lord Merlin."—*Illustrated News.* " Lord Merlin is a character which Farren should have played, and which, in his hands would have taken

Here I must take leave of Mr. Farren, who has hitherto carried me a little out of my course; just as in the first instance he unwittingly diverted the comedy from its original destination. But I could not dispense with him. He is as inseparable from the narrative of the comedy's adventures, as from the comedy itself. I cannot divorce him from either; and I have really some doubts, whether, in this new edition, considering the influence he has silently exercised over the play, I ought not to blot out the name of *Lord Merlin* from the *dramatis personæ*, and substitute Mr. Farren's in its place.

But, before we return to our *moutons*, let me protest against any misunderstanding touching this gentleman. Every actor has a right, for all I know to the contrary, to decline any or every part proposed to him. This is a matter I have nothing to do with; it belongs to the vital politics and managerial economy of the green room. It is obvious, however, than when an actor does decline a part, he invites criticism upon so responsible an exercise of his judgment. There may be, and often is, a profounder know-

its proper place in the comedy."—*Argus.* " Mr. Vandenhoff appears in a character written for Farren ; or so suitable to the powers of that actor, that it is only matter of regret the public could not see him in it." —*Satirist.* " Had Farren played Lord Merlin, and C. Matthews Sandford, the incongruity between the manners of the actors, and the language of the writer would not have been so apparent."—*Sunday Times.* " Mr. Farren ' could not see himself in it,' as the player's phrase runs, and re-fused the part. ＊ ＊ If Mr. Farren could really ' see himself,' although we acknowledge his great talents, he would give up at least one-third of the characters he is in the habit of performing. ＊ ＊ ' Mothers and Daughters' was cheerfully accepted by the manager of the Haymarket Theatre, and would have been produced there but for the unwarrantable egotism of Mr. Farren. Its merits were at once ac-knowledged at Covent Garden Theatre, and the only obstacle it had to encounter was the want of actors to do them justice."—*John Bull.* We might easily accumulate similar opinions, but *cui bono ?*

ledge of art concealed under rejected suggestions, than we find displayed in fulfilled designs. The question is at once raised in such a case as this. The actor may have a right to refuse a part; but public opinion has a right to examine and decide upon the propriety of that refusal. His refusal becomes just as much a matter of criticism in art, as his acceptance. It affects the result no less in an opposite direction, and generally a great deal more. It is enough for me to confine myself to the simple fact of Mr. Farren's inability to see himself in *Lord Merlin,* and the inability of the public to see anybody else in it. Mr. Farren may have a clear right to reject or select; and yet, like many other great men, may not always avail himself of his right rightly. In this instance, the public have plainly declared that he used his right wrongly.

The only revenge I desire is, that he may speedily be able to resume those efforts in which the errors of his judgment are not so easily detected. The loss of the public—who sadly miss his triumphant chuckle over the footlights, with the tails of his coat dancing on the tips of his fingers—is much greater than mine.

Let us now conduct the comedy with all due honours into the green-room. The company are assembled. Mr. Bartley reads the play. Every body concerned entertains the stranger with the most cordial good-will. All the scenes tell successfully (a good omen) on the habitual nerves of the listeners. The parts are cast and distributed; and the pleasant group, with their various fluctuating anticipations, break up like a flight of birds. This was on Saturday, January 14th, 1843.

To those who are acquainted with the preparations requisite for putting a five-act comedy on the stage, with any reasonable hope of success, it is needless to observe that some little time is necessary for study, and for such a number of rehearsals as will enable the performers not only to master the *finesse* of the dialogue (to say nothing about character), but to acquire a certain degree of fluency in its delivery—that fluency which is the life-blood of acted comedy. But to those who are not familiar with stage mysteries, it may be as well to add, that the time usually consumed in these preliminaries (as essential for the actors as the author), is about a month or six weeks, according to circumstances. In France, where these matters are much better ordered, a still longer period is devoted to this purpose.

Some notion of the care that was bestowed upon this comedy, may be formed from the circumstance, that it had FOUR rehearsals between the day when it was read in the green-room, and the night of its production on the stage ; and some of these rehearsals, too, were scrambled for amongst a mob of people who were trying to hurry forward in the same helter-skelter way, a tumultuous opera of such multitudinous magnificence, that it must have put the printer to his wits' end to squeeze its descriptive particulars into a double play-bill ! To suppose that any actors could be ready to do justice to a new play, or to themselves, at such short notice, would be preposterous ; but in this case, where some of the characters did not sit quite easily upon the performers, the utmost that could be hoped for, was to escape a complete and disgraceful failure. How much praise, then, is due to the artists who, under such circumstances, carried the play triumphantly through its perilous ordeal ?

" Mothers and Daughters" was produced on Tuesday, 24th January, and the play-bill of that day was filled with announcements *up to the following Saturday.* This is a significant feature in the case. If Mr. Bunn intended to give the comedy the smallest chance of success, he would have left room for its repetition, while the impression it made was yet fresh. But he never intended that it should succeed ; for reasons like those which made Dr. Johnson sleep without a night-cap—reasons which shall never be revealed to the remotest posterity, and which nobody will ever take the trouble to inquire into.

The representation was entirely successful. All the newspapers, with their infinite shades of critical opinion, agreed upon this point.* The reception was in the highest degree

* I have no desire to gather a bundle of laudatory criticisms from the newspapers, but simply to call witnesses, as a part of the case, in proof of the assertion that the play was entirely successful. "The piece was announced for repetition amidst considerable applause."—*Times.* "There was a great deal of applause, both during the performance of the comedy and at the conclusion, when Mr. Vandenhoff and the author were called for."—*M.Chronicle.* "The comedy commanded the most favourable attention of the house throughout its whole trial; it frequently drew down very general peals of laughter, and on the fall of the curtain its repetition was announced amid very warm plaudits. This was followed by a call for the author," &c.—*M. Herald.* "Each act, nay, several of the scenes in each were followed by an *encore* of enthusiastic applause. The curtain descended amid loud and general applause."—*M. Advertiser.* "The play went off with great applause."—*M. Post.* "At the fall of the curtain the applause was universal. The piece was one of the best comedies that has been produced of late years."— *Sun.* "Running over hastily in our minds the comedies which have been produced during the present century, we cannot think of one superior as a whole to this. It was well received throughout," &c.—*Britannia.* "The play went off with great applause."—*W. Chronicle.* "The audience were perfectly pleased. It was given out for repetition with much applause."—*Observer.* "The author was compelled to bow from his box amidst unanimous approbation."—*Illustrated London News.* "The merits of this work prevailed over circumstances, and it went triumphantly to a close. The applause during the fourth act was continuous. At the announcement for repetition the cheering gratifying to everybody—except the manager. He was the only dissentient in the house.

Mr. Bunn arrived just before the close of the performance. He was in time for the clamorous applause that crowned the final efforts of the performers; and before he retired from his box, the play—agreeably to the arrangements previously made—*was announced for repetition on the following Saturday.* The audience were evidently taken by surprise at such an extraordinary and unprecedented postponement of a successful drama, and cried out for its repetition on the following night. Their enthusiasm was drowned by the fiddles.

It might, perhaps, be said, that the play-bill ought not to be taken as conclusive evidence of the manager's intention not to repeat the comedy before Saturday, as he could have easily displaced the entertainments announced for the intervening nights, had the reception of the comedy seemed to him such as would warrant him in doing so; but it is quite clear that he really did not mean to displace those entertainments under any circumstances, simply because he did not leave his box until the stage-manager had already acted upon the arrangement laid down in the bill, so that he could not have averted the fulfilment of that arrangement, unless, like Sir Boyle Roche's bird, he could have been in two places at once.

The comedy was found too lengthy in representation, and the following Thursday was appointed for the purpose of effecting the necessary curtailments, *the company being called together by Mr. Bunn for that purpose.*

In the meanwhile, the playbill of Wednesday was issued

was very great."—*Argus.* "The applause was enthusiastic and general."—*Sunday Times.* "The piece was announced for repetition amidst considerable applause."—*Sentinel.* This is surely enough to show that at least the comedy succeeded.

c

with this announcement: "The New Comedy of 'Mothers and Daughters' having been successful, will be repeated on the following Saturday." Here at least was an acknowledgment, churlish enough to be sure, that the comedy *was* successful. On Wednesday, however, some new light broke in upon the manager, and the playbill of Thursday came out with this startling advertisement, in place of that which had previously appeared: "The new and successful Comedy of 'Mothers and Daughters' will be repeated three times a week." Here then was a comedy postponed for four days after its first appearance, and in the interval announced for repetition three times a week; as if, during the period of its withdrawal, it had somehow contrived to increase its power of attraction. But the flattering promise of the playbill was only designed to hoax the public—not the author. I was very soon undeceived. It was evident from an interview I had with Mr. Bunn on the Thursday, that he was in the meshes of a dilemma of his own creating; and that he would have acted more candidly if he had never announced the comedy for repetition at all — more honestly, if he had never put it into rehearsal. It was plain to see that he had calculated all along on the failure of the play; that he had, so to speak, made a sort of provision for its failure; that he was disappointed by its success, for which, in fact, he had made no provision; and that, expert as he is in strategy, he really did not know how to extricate himself from this comical embarrassment. There was clearly nothing to be done in the way of argument: sundry expedients were thrown out, but they were dispersed like dust in a whirlwind; and so the interview ended, Mr. Bunn promising to communicate with me as soon as he had resolved upon his plans.

I never heard from Mr. Bunn again. I might have waited till Doomsday, had I waited for any further communication.

The announcement that the comedy would be repeated three times a-week, remained in the bills on Thursday, Friday, and Saturday. On Monday, it was changed to " Due notice will be given of the next performance of the Comedy of 'Mothers and Daughters.' " This " due notice" is still " due." For three or four days longer, the amiable fiction was republished ; and then the name of the comedy was finally dropped out altogether.

If this were a matter simply between the author and the manager, I should certainly let the play glide quietly into oblivion, like a bubble on the waters, that had just glanced for a moment in the sunshine, and then suddenly drifted into shadow. But it is a matter of rather a wider reach — it involves the interests of all future dramatic writers, and through them the interests of dramatic literature itself ; and it also involves the right of the public to insist upon having their verdicts respected. When a play is damned, the author suffers in proportion : shall he not have the benefit of success ? I am well aware that all questions of this nature become more or less evasive, in the attempt to define and fix the responsibility ; but the fact of responsibility on general grounds is indisputable, while its extent and exaction must depend upon the special circumstances of each case.

The substantive question here is this : Whether a manager is justified in withdrawing a play which the public has approved, and the success of which, on its first representation, he has himself acknowledged in his bills ?

I felt that, even if I were indifferent to the assertion of

any personal reputation involved in the sudden death of a successful play, *this was a question I had no right to compromise.* It appeared to me that an obvious principle of common justice had been recklessly violated, and that I should be in some sort *particeps criminis* if I submitted to it. To acquiesce in a wrong is to confirm and consummate it. I resolved not to submit, but to bring this question to issue at any sacrifice.

In vain I endeavoured to ascertain why the comedy was thus unnaturally interred, while it was literally drawing its first breath, full of hope and vitality; the printed copy alone surviving to mourn, like Corneille's princess, over its buried half—

> Pleurez, pleurez mes yeux, et fondez vous en eau,
> La moitié de ma vie a mis l'autre au tombeau.

It was insinuated that the real cause was the smallness of the receipts. We have heard that Tenterden steeple is the cause of Goodwin's Sands. Whoever believes the one may believe the other. The comedy was withdrawn, and the British public was invited to witness, in its place, the highly-popular entertainments of " Rob Roy" and " Gustavus"— an invitation which the British public had the bad taste to decline. If the manager wished to have had the whole house to himself, he could not have devised a more ingenious expedient; and night after night he certainly had it all to himself.

But if the receipts were small—what had that to do with the comedy? It is not by the amount of the receipts the fate of a play is determined, but by the amount of applause. It has grown up almost into a theatrical proverb now-a-days, that first nights are not productive. People seem to wait to hear the result before they peril their money.   We have Mr. Bunn's own authority for the fact, that he always distributed three or four hundred free admissions on the first *three* or *four* nights of Mr. Sheridan Knowles' new plays.*   Now, the admissions issued on the first night of " Mothers and Daughters" bore no comparison with this costly outlay—yet the house was full, and the receipts were equal to the best nights of that unfortunate season†.   It may be a comfort, however, to all dramatic writers, to know that the receipts of a theatre have nothing to do with the matter in contract between them and the manager.   As their bargain is in no way improved by the largeness of the receipts, so it is in no way impaired by their smallness.   This is at least good equity and good common sense, and it was decided not many years ago to be good law, which is better than either, so far as material interests are concerned‡.

But, grant the argument that the receipts were low, and that, for that reason, the manager was justified in withdrawing the piece.   What then?   Did he withdraw it? No.   He announced it for repetition over and over again, and never repeated it.   Had he at once withdrawn it, on any pretence, I am not sure that, however unjust such a measure might have been, I should have had any remedy.

This miserable pretext, therefore, about the receipts, goes for nothing.   It might be a very good pretext, if it had any actual foundation in truth or usage; like the theory which makes the earth stand upon the back of a tortoise, and which might be a very good theory, if it

* On the trial of Gregory, *v*. the Duke of Brunswick.

† " The house was full."—*M. Chronicle*.   " The house was excessively well filled."—*Sun*.   " The author made a bow from a private box to a very full house."—*Weekly Dispatch*.   ‡ Jerrold *v*. Morris.

could only be shown that the tortoise itself had any thing to stand upon.

I must do Mr. Bunn the justice to say that he did not seem to know exactly what it was I wanted him to do. He did not seem to be aware that it was necessary to do any thing. He seemed to expect that an overture of some kind should come from me; and it did come from me at last, when all reasonable patience was fairly exhausted. It had begun, as the papers say, to furnish occupation for the " gentlemen of the long robe." Literature ought to stand clear of such associations—as long as it can. But there are cases in which, for its own sake, it becomes necessary to appeal to sterner tribunals than those of taste or opinion. This was precisely such a case. I have a great horror of law—but a still greater horror of injustice.

My object was not to recover pecuniary damages from Mr. Bunn, but to vindicate the principle he had outraged. This vindication would have been complete in the re-production of the comedy, and its repetition for a few nights, simply to show that a play which was successful on its first representation is entitled to a longer trial and a further test. I gave this alternative to Mr. Bunn, and at last he embraced it; but by a very remarkable coincidence, just as he agreed to re-produce the comedy, the theatre was suddenly shut up by the proprietors!

Nothing now remained but to remove it from " Common-Garden " to the Common Pleas. While the necessary steps were taking for this purpose, I was informed that there was a prospect of one of the large houses coming into Mr. Bunn's hands in the winter—that the pear was in fact ripening for him—and that in such an event, he would at once bring out the comedy. I was very willing to abide

the issue, and waited patiently. The pear ripened sure
enough, and Mr. Bunn became lessee of Drury Lane.
Now was the time for the redemption of his undertaking
But, unless it were to be set to music, or reduced to a
ballet of action, there was no earthly visible means by which
this play—embracing only about ten characters—could be
represented at the great national establishment,

Where Garrick trod and Grisi lives to dance.

Of course, all expectation was now at an end; and
Mr. Bunn, being unable to produce the comedy, which
he professed himself exceedingly anxious to do, offered to
make a statement to that effect, in which the principle I
sought to establish should be clearly acknowledged; con-
firming this acknowledgment and submission by relin-
quishing all claim upon the acting right in the comedy, and
by paying, in addition to all the legal expenses incurred, a
small sum towards the cost of publication. As I have a
strong aversion to settling by law any matters that can be
as effectually and more simply adjusted by reason, and as
this statement explicitly grants the whole question at issue,
so that the case can never be referred to hereafter as a precedent to the injury of others, I made no hesitation in ac-
cepting the proposed *amende*. I believe I have rendered
better service to the interests of dramatic literature in ac-
cepting this statement, than I could have done by making
a hostile demonstration in a court of law, by which I might
have obtained a larger personal indemnification, but with a
less satisfactory admission of the general principle at stake.

With this statement I bring the narrative to a conclusion,
and take leave of the subject without further commentary.
The only liberty I have used with Mr. Bunn's letter is the
omission of two or three complimentary phrases, which shed

a sort of opal light upon the transaction without making it a whit more clear. This letter was addressed to my solicitor.

> "*Theatre Royal, Drury Lane.*
> "*Jan.* 3, 1844.

"My Dear Sir,

"Regretting, as I do, the disappointment created by the non-repetition of Mr. Bell's comedy of 'Mothers and Daughters,' I beg to repeat that it arose from no want of merit in the comedy itself (of which I entertain the same opinion I have ever expressed, that it is one of our best of modern comedies), but is entirely to be attributed to the crippled state of the theatre, and the impossibility of doing it justice by those means which previous failures had left in my hands.

"The best opinion I can give you of Mr. Bell's comedy is, that I would have done it this season at Drury Lane, if I possessed a company capable of doing it justice.

"I am most happy in putting an end to the litigation between Mr. Bell and myself, by the payment of £50 towards the expenses incurred by Mr. Bell in printing the comedy, as well as his legal expenses, and of ceding to him the entire right of representing that comedy.

"I do this, not merely to express my sense of Mr. Bell's forbearance throughout all the unpleasantry which has arisen, but my highest appreciation of his gentlemanly conduct, &c., &c.

"If I knew how, either to Mr. Bell himself, or to the merits of his comedy, I could offer higher tribute, I would do so.

> "Yours, &c.
> "A. Bunn."

"J. Abbott, Esq.,
&c. &c.

For the civilities expressed in this letter, I hope I know how to be thankful; but Mr. Bunn would have better gratified my ambition by acting the comedy.

As it is, the Reader—gracious and courteous, I hope, and benignant, even, after this peaceful settlement of a very belligerent affair—is entreated to remember that the work he is here solicited to read was written with a direct view to the stage. This intention makes a material difference in the treatment—a difference, indeed, so material, that it is ten to one whether a comedy designed expressly for representation can afford much pleasure of a high kind in the closet.

Under any circumstances, an English comedy ought to be received with reasonable indulgence. The attempt, always attended with great difficulties, is now more difficult than ever. Both the stage and the people are out of joint for this sort of production in its pure integrity. People are growing too carped with care—too worldly—too sectarian for the gauds of the playhouse. And you cannot carve Closet Comedies out of the maxims of political economy, doctrinal discussions, or the traditions of the Tract Societies. Be gentle, then, O Reader, with this comedy, which, intended for the Stage, is condemned to haunt the Earth for a time in the shape of a Book; receive it less for what it is than for what it might have been; and, since Mr. Bunn would not act it, confer upon the author the immortal satisfaction of acting it yourself—that is to say, mentally, not corporeally. He only laments that he cannot supply you, in addition to the Book, with a complete mental wardrobe, and a superb suite of intellectual interiors to help out the flattering illusion !

d

MOTHERS AND DAUGHTERS.

ACT I.

SCENE I.

A magnificent apartment at LORD MERLIN'S. *Various works of art scattered about.* LOOP *discovered at a table looking over some books of plates.*

LOOP.

WELL, his lordship *has* taste. To be sure it may not be his own. A man with plenty of money can buy taste, just as he buys style.

Enter TOM.

TOM.

Mr. Cushion, the upholsterer—

LOOP.

Gently—gently—I am in no hurry. Well—

TOM.

Well—Mr.—Cushion—is—below—and—wants—to see you—Mr. Loop.

LOOP.

Too fast—too fast—now just go back, and deliver the message again.

TOM.

But Mr. Cushion is waiting below.

LOOP.

Quite right. Do you suppose I would see him the moment he's announced? Now, then—

TOM.

Mister Cushion, the upholsterer—

LOOP.

You want dignity, Tom. Stand here and observe me. (*Goes out and re-enters carelessly.*) Mr. Cushion, the upholsterer, wishes to see you, sir.

TOM.

Let him wait.

LOOP.

Eh?

TOM.

You don't suppose I'd see the fellow the very moment he calls, do you?

LOOP.

Very well!—ha!—Really Tom, you play the master better than the servant.

TOM.

So do you, Mr. Loop. It's far easier! But you wouldn't have me stand so, when I'm speaking to my lord, surely?

LOOP.

Why not, Tom? Never grovel—always look independent.

TOM.

Independent! How does that stand to reason? I'm only a servant.

LOOP.

Well?

TOM.

Well! I'm dependant on my lord.

LOOP.

Simpleton! my lord is dependant on you. A lord can do nothing for himself. He's a bundle of wants, that are supplied by his valet, his butler, his footman, and the rest of *us*. My philosophy is above you. Show Mr. Cushion up. Gently, Tom, gently. (*Exit* TOM.) Tom's a fool.

Enter MR. CUSHION *followed by* TOM.

LOOP.

You may go, Tom—there, slowly!   [*Exit* TOM. Cushion, how d'ye do?

CUSHION.

I hope you are very well, Mr. Loop.

LOOP.

Any thing fresh to-day, Cushion?

CUSHION.

Business, Mr. Loop, as usual, is very low.

LOOP.

Ha! good! Business is always—very low!

CUSHION.

No money to be had anywhere.

LOOP.

What do people want with money? Can't they live on credit?

CUSHION.

Ah! that's very well for the gentry, Mr. Loop; but we who provide them must get money somehow. Here is a case in point. The splendour of this house is not exceeded in London—furniture *à la Louis quatorze*—stained glass— verde antique—velvet screens—two statues of Venus—a bronze Apollo—

LOOP.

That will do—that will do—

CUSHION.

I beg pardon, Mr. Loop; I merely wished to say, that the outlay is very large, and I have put the account in my pocket, hoping you will submit it to his lordship.

LOOP.

Cushion, I believe I introduced you to his lordship to furnish this house.

CUSHION.

You did, Mr. Loop.

LOOP.

Now, do you suppose I should have done so, if I had had the least suspicion that you would trouble his lordship with an account before it was called for?

CUSHION.

Mr. Loop!

LOOP.

If the thing were known, you'd lose every customer you have in the world. It's fortunate it has happened with a friend like me; otherwise you might have been paid your account, and ruined for life.

CUSHION.

But, then—

LOOP.

Listen.   You are aware that Lord Merlin has only just come into the title—that he was only fourth, or fifth, cousin to the late lord, and never dreamt of such a piece of good luck.   In one hour he was transformed from a sneaking private gentleman reading the newspapers to keep out of the way of expense, and dining *à la carte* at his club, into a peer of the realm, with 25,000*l.* a-year.

CUSHION.

Yes, Mr. Loop.

LOOP.

Now, do be silent, Cushion.   Such a windfall at fifty or sixty years of age does not fall to a man every day.   I saw the advantages of his lordship's position, and, through private interest, secured the post of confidence I enjoy. His lordship and I are inseparable.   Having been a bachelor all his life, he has certain crude notions of the world, which it is my province to weed.   Indeed, he has hitherto lived on so paltry an income that, without my help, he never could get through half his fortune.

CUSHION.

I believe it, Mr. Loop.

LOOP.

I can easily manage his lordship; but Blount, his old man of all-work, who has lived with him all his life, and follows him like his shadow—it is not so easy to manage him.   Blount's an impracticable bear.

CUSHION.

Mr. Blount's a hard man, but very honest.

LOOP.

Honest!   I shall begin to have a very small opinion of
your understanding if you talk in that way.   Honest!
Is it likely you'd be upholsterer to a lord had you been an
honest man?   No—you'd have been a second-hand dealer
in broken chairs, camp-beds, and painted wash-hand
stands.   As to Blount, he'll never realize a farthing out of
my lord, nor let any body else if he can help it.   He's as
accurate in his accounts as the dumb register at Waterloo-
bridge, and is so incorrigibly conscientious, that I find it
impossible to keep on gentlemanly terms with him.   He's
sadly in my way, that's the truth.   You may leave your
account, but I cannot submit it to his lordship at present.

CUSHION.

But I have bills to make up—

LOOP.

They must wait.   It's a curious coincidence that every
tradesman I have had any thing to do with, has always
had bills to make up.   You and they must wait.   By the
way, have you furnished that little villa for me on the river?

CUSHION.

Every room;—it's quite a *bijou*.

LOOP (*confidentially*).

Is she perfectly satisfied with it?

CUSHION.

She says if you were a lord, you could not have acted
more handsomely.

LOOP.

What's the expense?

CUSHION.

Only ninety pounds, Mr. Loop.

LOOP.

Ninety pounds!   You said you'd charge me next to nothing.

CUSHION.

So I have.   I've included it in my lord's bill under the head of sundries.

LOOP.

Only ninety pounds?   It's too little.   Make it a hundred, and call on Thursday.

CUSHION.

I'm greatly obliged, Mr. Loop.   (*Aside*) The unblushing assurance of the puppy takes away my breath.   (*Going.*)

LOOP.

Cushion! the usual per centage, of course, is understood.

CUSHION.

Oh, certainly!   Good morning, Mr. Loop.   I remain ever your debtor.   (*Aside*) That puppy is a promising candidate for the Old Bailey.   [*Exit.*

LOOP.

Cushion's an ass!   He remains my debtor!   I'm his debtor, and intend to continue so.

LORD MERLIN (*outside*).

Loop!   Blount!

LOOP.

That's my lord.   Old habits will break out; he expects me to be in as great a hurry as he is himself.   (*Drawlingly*) Yes, my lord.

LORD MERLIN (*outside*).

Loop! Blount! (*Entering*) Is there nobody up yet?
What's the reason I'm not attended to?

LOOP.

My lord.

LORD MERLIN.

My lord! That's right. When I presume to call for any
thing, I'm answered with my lord! Yes, my lord! but
not a finger is stirred for all that. My fine gentleman
deliberates over every movement lest he should disturb
his tie, or the curve of his waistcoat.

LOOP.

My lord!

LORD MERLIN.

There again! I can't bear it! I never was hot; my
blood is naturally cool, regular, calm ; but now my pulse is
at ninety—it boils and gallops and—Loop! (*As* LOOP *is
going to speak interrupts him.*) Don't say, my lord! I'm
sick of it. I can buy a chorus of " my lords" for a shower
of halfpence. Loop, you've a good berth here—a capital
berth! I know many a gentleman—ay, sir, men born
and lapped in gentleness, who drudge hard by day and
night, for less than you get here for doing nothing. Look
to it.

LOOP.

I assure you, my lord.

LORD MERLIN.

You've too much assurance. Don't answer me. Get
me my letters.

LOOP (*aside, going over to a table for the letters*).
His lordship's a— hem!

LORD MERLIN.

Any cards this morning?

LOOP.

No, my lord.

LORD MERLIN.

Order the carriage at two o'clock.

LOOP.

'Tis already ordered at four, my lord.

LORD MERLIN.

Who ordered it at four?

LOOP.

Mr. Sandford, my lord.

LORD MERLIN.

Without consulting me! He's the only friend I have who is not altered towards me since I jumped into a title. Some flatter me—some are afraid of making too free. Bob's as impudent as ever! He shall inherit every sixpence I have. The worst of it is he knows it; and even that doesn't alter him. Ring the bell for Blount. Where's Mr. Sandford now?

LOOP.

Engaged in a rowing-match, my lord.

LORD MERLIN.

A rowing-match! How did he go?

LOOP.

In one of Newman's drags, my lord.

LORD MERLIN.

Humph! And not unlikely to come home by one of the Humane Society's. I hate water-parties!

Enter TOM.

LOOP.

Tom, tell Mr. Blount, his lordship wishes to see him.

[*Exit* TOM.

LORD MERLIN.

Bob does exactly what he likes, which is more than I can do, hedged in as I am by responsibilities of position. Position ! Commoners don't know how happy they ought to be. Loop, get me my brown coat.

LOOP.

My lord !

LORD MERLIN.

Mm— well ?

LOOP.

It is impossible your lordship can wear either the colour or the cut.

LORD MERLIN.

Why so ?

LOOP.

Out of date ; besides, animated by a profound zeal in your lordship's service, I have put it out of the way.

LORD MERLIN (*aside*).

His profound zeal, I suspect, is on intimate terms with the Jews. Rascal !—

Enter BLOUNT.

Well, Blount, have you been to the sale ?

BLOUNT.

Yes.

LORD MERLIN.

Well, and bought the Greek Phœnix ?

BLOUNT.

No.

LORD MERLIN.

What do you mean, Blount?

BLOUNT.

What do you want with a Greek Phœnix?

LORD MERLIN.

The great sale at Cherry Hill—the collection of *virtù* made by the late Lord Fillagree—every body insisted on my purchasing the Greek Phœnix, the famous Greek Phœnix,—it would look so well amongst my statues—I send you to buy it at any price—and you have the impudence—is it sold?

BLOUNT.

Yes.

LORD MERLIN.

Who bought it?

BLOUNT.

A fool.

LORD MERLIN.

Blount, you and I must separate.

BLOUNT.

No we shan't.

LORD MERLIN.

Upon what grounds do you presume to say so?

BLOUNT.

Upon a faithful service of forty years.

Enter SIR GREGORY PLUMP, *shown in by* TOM, *who remains.*

LORD MERLIN.

Gregory, you've just arrived in time to rescue me from a serious dilemma. I'm in a cleft stick between two servants. This gentleman is animated by such profound zeal in my service, that he won't let me wear a brown coat;

and this fellow, presuming upon forty years' fidelity, won't suffer me to buy Lord Fillagree's Greek Phœnix. This fellow is my man of business, and this, my man of pleasure. It seems I am to have no will of my own between them; a very pretty specimen of an unmarried nobleman's *ménage* at five-and-fifty!

BLOUNT.

Nothing more to say to me?

(LORD MERLIN *turns away to speak to* SIR GREGORY.)
[*Exit* BLOUNT—*a short pause.*

LOOP (*with an air of affectation*).

You may go, Tom.

LORD MERLIN.

So may you, sir.

TOM (*aside to* LOOP *as he is going out*).

Gently, Mr. Loop—gently!
[*Exeunt* TOM *and* LOOP.

SIR GREGORY PLUMP.

Well, if you're not the happiest of mankind, you're certainly the most fortunate.

LORD MERLIN.

I suppose I must submit to be thought so. I hear they've already got up a *sobriquet* for me at the clubs. Now, Gregory, you've known me nearly fifty years—what do you think they call me at the clubs?

SIR GREGORY PLUMP.

I can't say.

LORD MERLIN.

Why they call me the fortunate youth!

SIR GREGORY PLUMP.

Ha! ha! ha!

LORD MERLIN.

Ha! ha! Pleasant that! Because I have unexpectedly inherited a title and estates. Gregory, the clubs are hot-beds of vanity, jealousy, and selfishness. I know them well. I have lived all my life in a club, and I never made a friend in it. I know five hundred faces intimately that I meet there every day—but I never was able to detect an expression of sympathy in one of them. Men get hardened in clubs—isolated—and insincere, and learn to regard familiar faces with apathy, to the utter annihilation of the finest instincts of nature.

SIR GREGORY PLUMP.

There are exceptions, my friend; yourself for example.

LORD MERLIN.

Perhaps. They haven't made me cold and venemous—but they have made me look into myself, and know myself better. They have taught me to enjoy the world; and I mean to enjoy it. I'm just going to begin life, Gregory.

SIR GREGORY PLUMP.

Why just now you confessed to five-and-fifty.

LORD MERLIN.

What of that? I have a noble fortune;—no less than 25,000*l.* per annum—an estate in Buckingham—and a title. These are the elements of the fashionable alchemy that enables age to put on the spring-tide airs of youth. Why, man, half the women will be running after me when I make my *début (with gaiety).* I'm only just coming out.

SIR GREGORY PLUMP.

And will make as good a figure as the youngest of them—only I'm afraid, between ourselves, that neither you nor I, can keep up the ball quite as merrily as we might, have done some twenty or thirty years ago.

LORD MERLIN.

Speak for yourself, Gregory. Perhaps you've hurt your constitution—I've taken care of mine. I've been pent up on a scanty annuity, and had no vent for my animal spirits.

SIR GREGORY PLUMP.

So much the worse. You're not used to excitement, and a sudden plunge into gay life will disorganize you.

LORD MERLIN.

You never committed a greater mistake. My love of pleasure has been bottled up, and I'm only going to take out the cork. How my champagne nature will fly! I've been a clubman all my life. I lived in the club; the library was my room—it was inexpensive. I lived within myself—it made me sullen. I nearly lost the use of my tongue. My utmost luxury was a white horse, and a livery-servant—three hundred yards off, regulation distance—on a fine day! But that's over. I'm coming out, Gregory!

SIR GREGORY PLUMP.

And you have taken your nephew, Bob Sandford, to live with you altogether?

LORD MERLIN.

Altogether. I hate solitude. I've had enough of it; Bob's a rattle-headed dog, with a fine spirit, an honest fellow. He'll help me to get through my fortune like a gentleman; and he shall inherit my estate when I'm gone.

SIR GREGORY PLUMP.

With such a prospect before him, I hope he will make a prudent settlement one of these days.

LORD MERLIN.

I hope he will do nothing of the kind. With such a prospect before him, he has no necessity for sordid calculations; I never knew a prudent settlement that didn't end in a break up.

SIR GREGORY PLUMP.

But he may make a foolish match.

LORD MERLIN.

He may make any match he pleases—provided I approve of it. Don't be afraid of Bob; the young men of the present day, Gregory, are a hundred fold more knowing than they were in our time. Rely upon it, the world don't turn round for nothing. But how goes on your suit with the widow? Any prospect of a prudent settlement there?

SIR GREGORY PLUMP.

I hardly know. Lady Manifold is so uncertain in her humours, and so engrossed moreover with projects for getting her silly daughter off her hands, that I never can obtain on opportunity of bringing her to an understanding. The fact is, I'm an old fool to trouble my head about her.

LORD MERLIN.

But are you sure it's about *her* you trouble your head? —quite sure it's not her jointure?

SIR GREGORY PLUMP.

Why, of course; but jointures, you know, can only be wooed through widows. Ah, my lord, I'm not lucky like you. The women keep clear of me. It's notorious that the last contest for Fishborough has crippled my estate. Now, by and by, the whole sex will be looking out for you.

LORD MERLIN.

My dear fellow, they're beginning to nibble already! and Lady Manifold herself's in the front rank. Don't be alarmed. She wants to marry me to her daughter—(for the sake of my fortune)—with a reversionary interest in my nephew. For fear of accident she's ogling us both at the same time; and I conscientiously believe she'd marry us both at the same time, if she could.

SIR GREGORY PLUMP.

Well, and what will come of it?

LORD MERLIN.

Nothing. By all accounts, for I have never seen her, the daughter's a half-simpleton. I have too much sense for her—Bob has too much blood.

SIR GREGORY PLUMP.

You don't know Lady Manifold's talents for intrigue. If she fail with you, she may succeed with your nephew.

LORD MERLIN.

Pshaw! She only furnishes us with amusement. Here's a letter inviting me to a rout for the 22d. She writes me a special note :—" My dear Lord—the happiness—hum !— ever—delight—your sincere Georgina Manifold,"—a special note—not a card such as she sends to every body else. Don't you suppose I can see through this, Gregory?

SIR GREGORY PLUMP.

All very well for a time; but, with such opportunities, you'll marry in the long run.

LORD MERLIN.

Marry!—no—not marry, Gregory. (*Slightly affected, but overcoming his feelings.*) The time is past—I'm old—there is rejuvenescence for every thing but the affections! There is no second youth of the affections! I can enjoy the world as well as ever—more wisely, certainly—ay, and as merrily as ever, Gregory,—why not? — but marry — no! — one wants heart for that — heart, heart, heart! Come, come, talk of something else.

SIR GREGORY PLUMP.

I have touched some old memory.

LORD MERLIN.

No—no.

SIR GREGORY PLUMP.

If I could have imagined—

LORD MERLIN.

Nonsense—it's very foolish, Gregory, for old fellows like us to be talking about such things.

[*They retire up the stage.*

Enter SANDFORD, *in a boating dress, with a letter in his hand.*

SANDFORD.

Charming—charming. The very thing I longed for, but did not dare to hope. That the old lady should invite me in so marked a manner. (*Reading*)—"Dear Mr. Sandford"—oh! precious, delightful old woman—"cannot do without you"—"your sincere Georgina Manifold"—and what a pretty name she has—Georgina! I wonder what my uncle would say if he knew this.

LORD MERLIN (*aside to* SIR GREGORY, *showing his letter*).

I wonder what my nephew would say if he knew this.

SANDFORD.

He hasn't the slightest notion of such a thing.

LORD MERLIN (*aside*).

You're wrong, Bob; he has a very clear notion of it.

SANDFORD.

" Cannot do without you "—nor I without you—

LORD MERLIN (*aside*).

Damn it, he's not in love with the old woman!

SIR GREGORY (*aside*).

I hope not.

SANDFORD.

The 22d. How long is it to the 22d. To touch her sweet hand again, and dream away an hour in her eyes!

SIR GREGORY PLUMP (*aside*).

No, that can't be Lady Manifold.

SANDFORD.

To hear her voice again!

LORD MERLIN (*aside*).

It must be her daughter. What fools these boys are, Gregory.

SANDFORD.

Such a delicious evening we shall have!

LORD MERLIN.

Shall you? The fellow is going to rival me in the girl's affections. I'll see. (*Comes forward*) Bob!

SANDFORD.

Pshaw!　Why do you startle one so?

LORD MERLIN.

Startle you, did I?　What were you reading just now?

SANDFORD.

Reading?—was I reading?

LORD MERLIN.

What was it?

SANDFORD.

Oh!—a—nothing!

LORD MERLIN.

Nothing! Eh! Bob?

SANDFORD.

Uncle, you've no right to be curious.

LORD MERLIN.

Nephew, you've no right to be mysterious.　It was a letter.

SANDFORD.

So it was.

LORD MERLIN.

You see, although I'm no conjurer, I can find out a secret.

SANDFORD.

No, you haven't found out the secret yet.

LORD MERLIN.

Yes, I have; it was from Lady Manifold.

SANDFORD.

Well, so far you're right; but you never could guess what it's about.

LORD MERLIN.

Couldn't I ?

SANDFORD.

Never ! never !

LORD MERLIN.

Her ladyship gives a rout on the 22d.

SANDFORD.

And I've got an invitation.

LORD MERLIN.

And I've got another.　(*Shows their letters.*)

SANDFORD.

You have ?

LORD MERLIN.

I have.　But, Bob, you mustn't be in my way.　If I catch you poaching—

SANDFORD.

But, uncle, you're not serious ?

LORD MERLIN.

Why not, sir ? my friend Sir Gregory Plump and I have monopolised the ladies between us, eh ! Gregory ? and if you interfere with either one or the other of them, you must make up your mind to the consequences.

SANDFORD.

Sir Gregory, is my uncle really in earnest ?

SIR GREGORY PLUMP.

Perfectly in earnest, Mr. Sandford.　I have undertaken to relieve your uncle from the old lady, that he may have more leisure for the young one.

SANDFORD.

The young one ?   What young one?

LORD MERLIN.

What young one ?   Pray, sir, is that the way you speak
of the mesmeric divinity whose eyes are to set you dreaming by the hour together ?   Dreaming !   Eyes had a different sort of magnetism in our day, Gregory.

SANDFORD.

Well, I acknowledge, I did rhapsodize a little ; but you
must confess, uncle, it was not fair to listen.

LORD MERLÌN.

Every thing is fair in love, Bob.

SANDFORD.

Love ! what does your lordship mean?

LORD MERLIN.

That if you attempt to attract the affections of Miss
Manifold by any of your rhapsodies, I'll break with you
for ever.

SANDFORD (*exultingly*).

Is that all ?

LORD MERLIN.

That's all.

SANDFORD.

Then, my dear uncle, I pledge you my honour I never
will ; and there's my hand on it.

LORD MERLIN.

You're an honest fellow.   Didn't I tell you, Gregory,
he had too much blood for her ?   Why of the two, Bob,
I'd rather you'd marry the old woman herself.

SIR GREGORY PLUMP.

Why, my lord, don't you see that's exactly what he intends?

LORD MERLIN.

Pooh!

SIR GREGORY PLUMP.

Pooh! But I tell you it is. He's in ecstasies about one of them—that's clear. It isn't the daughter—who then do you suppose it to be?

LORD MERLIN.

The inference is unanswerable, I admit. But I don't believe it.

SIR GREGORY PLUMP.

I'll put it beyond doubt. Mr. Sandford!

SANDFORD.

Sir Gregory Plump!

SIR GREGORY PLUMP.

In one word sir, have you any design upon Lady Manifold?

SANDFORD.

Lady Manifold?

SIR GREGORY PLUMP.

Yes, sir, Lady Manifold.

SANDFORD.

Lady Manifold!—ha!—ha!—ha!

SIR GREGORY PLUMP.

He's laughing at me.

LORD MERLIN.

I thought he would.

SANDFORD.

Excuse me for laughing, Sir Gregory, but the idea—design! ha! ha! ha!—no! no!

SIR GREGORY PLUMP.

Why to be sure, it wás very ridiculous.

SANDFORD.

You may make your mind easy, Sir Gregory. I don't think you have a rival in the world. Her ladyship is too clever to attract admirers. The men are afraid of her talents; and if you really mean to prosecute your suit, your motto must be *nil disperandum*.

LORD MERLIN.

You may take Bob's word, Gregory, for the state of affairs. He's a regular visiter at her ladyship's. By the way, perhaps you can tell us something about the daughter also.

SANDFORD.

Oh! she's a mere doll. Her mother has managed to keep her so completely out of the way of society—lest she might make a false step! that now she's out, she's ready to devour every man she meets.

SIR GREGORY PLUMP.

Or to be devoured by the first roaring lover who comes in her way. She has the airs of the boarding-school, without its discipline. If she had high romping spirits one might put up with her; but she's a poor die-away lacka-daisical moppet, without a particle of sense or feeling.

LORD MERLIN.

But, having the reputation of a fortune, I wonder some greedy needy hanger-on doesn't snap her up. A hungry devil who wasn't very nice might swallow her, affectation and all. Her money would make her go down palatably.

SANDFORD.

If I don't mistake there's a wolf's mouth open for the lamb already. I hear of a Captain Montague, a swaggering half-pay, as poor as a rat and as impudent as a beadle, who is on her trail night, noon, and morning. Lady Manifold has effectually scared off every body else, but hasn't a suspicion of the captain.

LORD MERLIN.

I hope he'll outwit her. I wish every manœuvring mother in the kingdom had a keen-witted fortune-hunter at her heels, to undo in the night the machinations her maternal genius had woven in the morning. Come, Gregory, you'll dine with me to-day, and we'll settle our plans over a glass of Burgundy. At our period of life, Gregory, when a man resolves upon a career of pleasure, he cannot afford to throw away a moment. Come along.

[*Exit with* GREGORY.

SANDFORD.

He has not the least suspicion. I am glad of it. Yet why should I be afraid to avow my attachment for Mabel? He is so frank and generous to me! I am sure he would be proud of Mabel, if he knew her. But stay, Master Bob—you're making rather a premature reckoning. Are you quite sure that Mabel will have you? I never thought of that! It never entered my wise head that Mabel might possibly refuse me.—No! that's impossible. But wouldn't it be just as well to ascertain the state of her feelings, before I run any risks with my uncle?—I'll do it— I'll do it

LORD MERLIN (*outside*).

Bob!

SANDFORD.

Yes, my lord—I'll go to her at once—

LORD MERLIN (*outside*).'

Bob—I say—

SANDFORD.

I'm coming, my dear uncle—It's a matter of life and death; I'll order the carriage instantly and be off. (*Rings the bell.*) Tom!

LORD MERLIN (*outside*).

Bob!

SANDFORD.

Coming, my lord—Tom!—Remember the old proverb, cups and lips—lips! her lips! damme, I'm gone. Tom!

[*Exit at the opposite side.*

LORD MERLIN (*outside*).

Bob!

(*Bell rings at both sides. The curtain drops.*)

END OF ACT I.

ACT II.

SCENE I.

Drawing-room, opening upon a suite of rooms lighted beyond, at Lady MANIFOLD'S. ROSE *peeps in from the back.*

ROSE.

Miss—Miss Emily—there's nobody here. Come in, miss—it's like one desert vast with idle ancles, as Othello says. Don't be afraid, miss.

Enter EMILY MANIFOLD, *timidly, with sidelong looks.*

EMILY MANIFOLD.

Oh! Rose, how my heart palpitates.

ROSE.

Well, miss, it was made to palpitate. La! it's as natural as possible. I only wish Captain Montague could see you now, miss; you do look so very languishing.

EMILY MANIFOLD.

Do you really think he loves me, Rose?

ROSE.

Oh! miss: love's not the word. It's fiery flames—intoxicating delirium—did you ever read the "Tears of Sensibility," miss?

EMILY MANIFOLD.

Never, Rose.

ROSE.

You ought, miss. It's very necessary. I should never

have known what love was, but for the "Tears of Sensibility," miss.

EMILY MANIFOLD.

But the captain, Rose. Didn't he give you a letter for me?

ROSE.

He did, miss. But my lady—

EMILY MANIFOLD.

My mother—

ROSE.

Found it on my table.

EMILY MANIFOLD.

Then every thing is discovered.

ROSE.

Oh! you are very simple, miss, begging your pardon. You don't suppose the captain wrote your name on it. No. It was addressed to the " Angel of my Life !" Now, my lady may think she's the angel of his life, if she pleases, and no harm done.

EMILY MANIFOLD.

Heigho! I'm not only likely to lose the man I love, but may be compelled to accept some wretch I loathe.

ROSE.

It's absolute weakness in mothers not to know that the man of their choice must naturally be odious to their daughters.

EMILY MANIFOLD.

There's Lord Merlin—he's the last fancy of my mother's : she supposes that because he's a peer, and has a fine fortune, I should be the happiest of wives. But, oh! Rose, what are titles and wealth compared to love?

ROSE.

Nothing, miss. You must write to the captain.

EMILY MANIFOLD.

Write to the captain! What would he think of my
delicacy?

ROSE.

Oh! miss, when one's in love they musn't stand upon
their delicacy. Look here, miss, I have written a letter
to the object of my affections! Obdurate Cupid—he's
insensible to my pangs—he's such a fine gentleman, miss.
If you won't betray my confiding nature, miss, I'll reveal
who he is.

EMILY MANIFOLD.

Well—

ROSE.

He is Mr. Loop, miss—confidential secretary to Lord
Merlin. Thousands pass through his hands every day.
Shall I read it, miss?

EMILY MANIFOLD.

Do, Rose.

ROSE (*reads*).

"Dearest, dearest, nameless one! I am the most miserable of women. I know what separates me from you—
not space or time, but some rival! I have told your fortune by the cards night after night. The cards tell me you
are inclined to make an offer to a dark young woman.
There is something about a child I can't make out. You
talked to her recently; she has money. Star of my night,
I know your sentiments by the cards. Come to me soon.
There is not a joy to charm unless shared with thee, nor is it
in fate to harm me, if fate will only leave me thy love. I
see thee not—I hear thee not—yet am present with thee,

albeit my brow thou shouldst never more behold. I should
very much like to be mistress of an hotel. It is the only
business I shall ever take up with. Believe me fit for
it, dearest. Thine. Thyrza!"

EMILY MANIFOLD.

Thyrza! that's not your name.

ROSE.

No, sure. I got it out of the "Tears of Sensibility." La!
Miss — there's your honoured mother! If she sees us
together—I'll run this way—you go that way.

> [*She runs off.*

Enter LADY MANIFOLD *at the back, meeting* EMILY *as she
is going out.*

LADY MANIFOLD.

Well, my dear, where are you running in such a hurry?

EMILY MANIFOLD.

Was I in a hurry, ma?

LADY MANIFOLD.

Don't be so scared, my dear. I declare one would
fancy that you had been doing some mischief in a corner,
child, you have such a frightened look. I have been
inquiring for you, Emily. I've got something very serious
to say to you.

EMILY MANIFOLD (*aside*).

Oh! dear.

LADY MANIFOLD.

Chairs, child (*Emily draws over chairs*). You know,
Emily, that ever since you were twenty-one—don't fidget
so with your fingers—I have thought it right, child, to

consider your settlement in life, love, as the principal
business—do, put away that tassel—I may safely say that
I have thought of scarcely any thing else.

EMILY MANIFOLD.

Nor I neither, ma !

LADY MANIFOLD.

That's not pretty, love. You've no business to think
about such things.

EMILY MANIFOLD.

But, ma—

LADY MANIFOLD.

Be silent, child. I know best what's for your welfare.
My anxiety to secure you a good match has rendered me
so cautious and circumspect, that—

EMILY MANIFOLD.

I have not had a single offer.

LADY MANIFOLD.

You talk like a simpleton. You don't suppose that the
people I encourage would venture to propose for you without my approbation. No, child; I am resolved that your
youth and simplicity shall have all the advantage in the
choice of a husband which they can derive from my observation and experience.

EMILY MANIFOLD.

But, ma, as my youth and simplicity have derived so
little advantage from your experience , isn't it almost time
that I should begin to look out for myself.

LADY MANIFOLD.

Mercy upon me, Emily; I never heard you make use

of such an expression before. Have you been reading any naughty books, child? Look out for yourself! Do you know what you are saying, love?

EMILY MANIFOLD.

Oh! yes.

LADY MANIFOLD.

Indeed you do not. You've got some crotchet into your head, and the sooner you get it out of your head the better. The idea of a young lady looking out for herself! Such innocence! My dear, I have brought you up so carefully, that you are quite ignorant of the world. Happy ignorance! You haven't a notion of the foolish things some girls of your age get thinking of—love and nonsense.

EMILY MANIFOLD (*aside*).

You're very much mistaken, though.

LADY MANIFOLD.

I was always against boarding-schools on that account. I preferred the domestic system; and it was for that reason, love, I admitted Mabel Trevor into my house. She is really, I believe, a very harmless creature, and makes an excellent sort of humble companion.

EMILY MANIFOLD.

Oh! she is very good.

LADY MANIFOLD.

Now, my dear, do you know why I've given this rout this evening?

EMILY MANIFOLD.

I'm sure I don't know, unless it's because you like it.

LADY MANIFOLD.

Well, that's an ingenuous answer at all events. I expect Lord Merlin, and his nephew, Mr. Sandford, here. My dear Emily, you don't know what sacrifices I have made to produce an effect upon his lordship.—That is a very handsome dress, and the colour suits your complexion sweetly; but hasn't Fleury been here with the wreath?

EMILY MANIFOLD.

No. She's a provoking wretch. I never would deal with her again.

LADY MANIFOLD.

You only want a dash of rich flowers at this side in your hair to make you perfect. Be sure to attend to it before Lord Merlin comes. You really look quite captivating, love.

EMILY MANIFOLD.

Do I? Will Captain Montague be here?

LADY MANIFOLD.

Captain Montague! Pooh! child. Poor Montague; that's all because he acts charades with you. How easily my innocent Emily is amused. Don't mind the Captain dear. Think of Lord Merlin, and his 25,000*l.* a-year. What would I have given for such a chance at your age. Now, mark: look at him always when he's not looking at you, and then, the moment he turns and sees you, drop your eyes and look confused.

EMILY MANIFOLD.

Oh! I know.

LADY MANIFOLD.

Don't be too eager to reply to him when he speaks to

you; and the less you say the better, lest you might commit yourself. Indeed, it's a prudent rule for a woman to trust every thing to her eyes, and nothing to her tongue. I found it answer most successfully.

EMILY MANIFOLD.

But, suppose he doesn't take any notice of me, may I talk to Captain Montague then, ma?

LADY MANIFOLD.

Oh! you may talk as much as you please to Montague. That's quite safe. Upon second thoughts, it would be an excellent plan to play off the hectoring captain against the polished aristocrat. His lordship might be piqued by your attention to a man so much his inferior in rank and fortune.

EMILY MANIFOLD.

I'm sure, ma, I'll do all in my power to pique him.

LADY MANIFOLD (rising).

And in any case, my dear, there is Mr. Sandford; he is to inherit every farthing of his lordship's wealth, and who knows but, should we miss the uncle, we may bring down the nephew. It's all the same, so far as the property is concerned; and Mr. Sandford has at least the advantage of being a few years younger. Now, run away, and put in the flowers.—I see the company is arriving. [Going up.

EMILY MANIFOLD.

And may I try to pique Mr. Sandford too, ma?

LADY MANIFOLD.

Oh! certainly, love! What an innocent child it is!
[Exit at the back.

D

EMILY MANIFOLD.

I'll take you at your word, you may depend upon it, my good mama! Oh! Montague, wherefore art thou Montague! or why art thou only a captain?

MONTAGUE (*who has just entered at the side*).

For thy sake, dearest, I would be a lord—if I could. But what is a lord? I'm richer than any lord in England.

EMILY MANIFOLD.

You are? Then ma will—(*stops herself suddenly*).

MONTAGUE.

Am I not richer in thy love than a thousand Merlins?

EMILY MANIFOLD.

Oh! Montague—You overheard me.

MONTAGUE.

I overheard only the beating of your heart. But I could hear that, if a mountain divided us, by the responsive ticking of my own. I know every thought that passes in your mind. How can it be otherwise when I am perpetually thinking of you? Love is a species of intuition that produces an incommunicable sympathy between two people predestined by nature for each other. I knew my fate the first moment I saw you; and it would have been just the same if I had never seen you. In the latter case, I must have gone about the world like the moiety of a human soul in search of my other half.

EMILY MANIFOLD.

Thatwould have been charming.

MONTAGUE.

But the reality is better than the dream.   You are mine already, by all the unspoken pledges in your eyes.—You must be mine by a licence.   When shall I have a carriage-and-four early in the morning at the corner of Hertford-street ?

EMILY MANIFOLD.

I am generally up about ten.

MONTAGUE.

But the whole town is up then—

EMILY MANIFOLD.

Hush ! Ma is determined I shall be married to Lord Merlin.

MONTAGUE.

And I'm determined you shall not.

EMILY MANIFOLD.

Oh ! that's beautiful ! He's to be here to-night.

MONTAGUE.

Ill sup on him !

EMILY MANIFOLD.

Delightful !   But ma says that I may talk as much as I please to you to pique him.

MONTAGUE.

She does?

EMILY MANIFOLD.

She doesn't mind you, she says. She thinks you're quite safe ; and she says it would be an excellent plan to play you off against his lordship.

MONTAGUE.

Did she say all this ?   Then I'll be played off to some
purpose ; I'll pop her into my " Life and Times."

EMILY MANIFOLD.

Your " Life and Times."   Gracious !

MONTAGUE.

Didn't you know I was writing my " Life and Times" ?
I put every body into it that does any thing out of the way.

EMILY MANIFOLD.

But ma shan't thwart me, I'm determined.   I'll have you
and nobody else.

> With thee content, I ask no more ;
> I want not lands, nor golden store,
> Nor furnished palaces—oh ! Jove,
> Give me but naked walls and love !

MONTAGUE.

You're a divinity.   (*Aside*) Lucky she likes *naked* walls.

EMILY MANIFOLD.

Here she is.   I'll stay with you the whole evening.
[*Runs over and takes* MONTAGUE'S *arm.*

Enter LADY MANIFOLD.

LADY MANIFOLD.

Ha ! Montague, are you come ?—Emily, child, what are
you doing there ?

EMILY MANIFOLD.

Only practising, ma—

LADY MANIFOLD.

Practising, my love ?

EMILY MANIFOLD.

Why, ma, you told me to play off Captain Montague against Lord Merlin, and so I'm getting the captain to rehearse with me a little before we go into the ball-room— that's all—

LADY MANIFOLD.

Emily, I'm astonished. How can you be so very absurd. I really believe you think it's one of your acted charades you're getting up.

EMILY MANIFOLD.

Oh! not at all. I'm quite in earnest.

LADY MANIFOLD.

Captain, you are a man of the world, and will readily understand—

MONTAGUE.

Oh! perfectly, madam.

LADY MANIFOLD.

My daughter's fortune is not quite a plum ; (*laughing*) and so good a match, you know, captain, ought not to be allowed to slip through one's fingers.

MONTAGUE.

Certainly not. And, in short, you wish to hasten it by seeming to throw a little impediment in the way ?

LADY MANIFOLD.

Why not exactly that; but, since my daughter *has* let you into our little family secrets, I can have no hesitation in saying, that it would be no harm if it appeared that she had other admirers—just to touch his lordship's vanity— for you know when a man arrives at a certain age he is not capable of being actually in love with any woman ; but there is no age at which he ceases to be in love with himself.   You can appreciate the anxiety of a mother about the happiness of an only daughter.   Just flirt a little in your own goodnatured way.—You know you're an universal flirt, Montague.

MONTAGUE.

Your ladyship is the very genius of intrigue.   I'll do it with alacrity—make love to your daughter before your face, and throw Lord Merlin over the bannisters if he utters a syllable.

LADY MANIFOLD.

There's his lordship in the next room.   I must receive him.   Now, my love, run and get ready.   Montague, will you remain here till I return ?

[EMILY *goes out at the side,* LADY MANIFOLD *at the back.*

MONTAGUE.

'Pon my life, I'm in a very agreeable predicament. But it's tolerably clear, I have the best of the dilemma. Her ladyship has thought proper to place me in a dangerous and rather equivocal relationship with her daughter, and she has no right to blame me for the consequences. Her daughter has thought proper to let me make love to her in downright reality, and has no right to blame me for the consequences either.   I am, consequently, free from all blame between them.   I'll pop them both into my " Life and Times."   Emily shall be the heroine—portrait in the second volume.

EMILY MANIFOLD (*peeping out at the side, fastening a wreath of flowers in her hair*).

Captain, remember it's for you I'm putting the flowers in my hair—not for Lord Merlin.

MONTAGUE.

Flower of Paradise—they're coming.

[EMILY *disappears ;* LADY MANIFOLD, LORD MERLIN
SIR GREGORY PLUMP, *and* MR. SANDFORD *come
down the stage.*

LADY MANIFOLD.

Your lordship argues with such consummate art, that
you almost convince my judgment against the evidence
of my senses.

LORD MERLIN.

And why not, my lady ? Your senses are not infallible
—but your ladyship's judgment is—(*aside*)—ahem !

LADY MANIFOLD.

In this instance, at least, since it bows implicitly to your
lordship.

LORD MERLIN.

Oh ! (*Aside*) A nibble, Gregory !

LADY MANIFOLD.

How d'ye do again, Montague ? My lord, Captain Montague—Lord Merlin, Sir Gregory Plump, Mr. Sandford.
There now, entertain each other for five minutes. I have
to chaperon my timid daughter into the drawing-room.
You would hardly believe it, my lord, but she is such an
inartificial and sensitive creature, that I am obliged to be
constantly at her side in public. Isn't she, Montague ?

MONTAGUE.

Remarkably so, your ladyship.

LADY MANIFOLD.

You would scarcely believe that of my daughter ?

LORD MERLIN.

Never should have suspected it, madam.

LADY MANIFOLD.

To sure this is only her first season. She was presented on Wednesday. But she is so natural—so unadulterated. Ah! my lord, he will be a happy man who gets her for a wife. [*Exit.*

LORD MERLIN.

Pretty plain that, Gregory.

MONTAGUE.

Hem!—my lord—enchanted to make your lordship's acquaintance. Often heard of you—extraordinary luck!— Fortunate youth!—Happy to know your friends, too; Sir Gregory Plump—your nephew, Mr. Sandford. All unmarried, I believe. Looking out for wives—eh?—So am I. Three characters! I'll pop you into my "Life and Times."

LORD MERLIN.

Sir—I haven't the honour—

MONTAGUE.

No matter—I'm writing my life—"Life and Times" —Swinford Hastings Montague—Reminiscences—Anecdotes.

SIR GREGORY PLUMP.

Has any thing very extraordinary happened to you that you should write your life?

MONTAGUE.

No—nothing.

LORD MERLIN.

No battles—no adventures? Have you run away with any body's wife?

MONTAGUE.

No; my life is singularly destitute of incidents. It has been passed principally between the end of Regent-street and Hyde-park-corner. But I am constantly upon town, and pick up all sorts of intelligence. Being an idle man, I'm at all the private views—have the *entrée* behind the scenes at the theatres—am intimate with most of the noted people—keep a journal—note down at night every thing I hear through the day.

LORD MERLIN.

And you think yourself quite justified in publishing to the world every careless observation you chance to " pick up" in society.

MONTAGUE.

Certainly; if it be any thing out of the way.

LORD MERLIN.

Then, sir, I hope you will particularly remember to note this remark, that the man who retails in print the heedless conversations of private life ought to be shunned as a viper. Like the rot in a ship, he undermines the social fabric without being felt or suspected, takes advantage of his admission to the domestic circle to violate domestic confidence, and having obtained his materials under false pretences, he lives by pandering them to the depraved appetites of the public.

MONTAGUE.

You must give me a copy of that. It's too long to remember.

Enter LADY MANIFOLD *and* EMILY *at the back.* MABEL TREVOR *appears slowly after them and lingers behind. As the conversation advances, the company gradually collect, forming groups in the background.*

LADY MANIFOLD.

We are so glad to escape the crowd and heat. My dear
lord, allow me to present you to my daughter. Lord
Merlin, love. She is so unused to such a crush, my lord.
Sir Gregory Plump, my dear, and his lordship's nephew,
Mr. Sandford, my love! Captain Montague—but you
know these gentlemen. She's so timid!

LORD MERLIN.

I should have known Miss Manifold amongst a thousand by her eyes and hair! quite the family beauty, your
ladyship.

LADY MANIFOLD (*aside to* EMILY).

Say you don't believe gentlemen when they flatter you.

EMILY MANIFOLD.

Oh! my lord, I don't believe gentlemen when they flatter me.

LORD MERLIN.

Then I confess, miss, speaking frankly, that what
nature has done for you, art has gone near to spoil. That
vile bunch of flowers ruins the delicacy of your complexion. There's no flattery in that. I hope you'll believe it.

LADY MANIFOLD (*interposing*).

Oh! my lord, you cannot expect her to believe that.

MONTAGUE.

In truth, no: for it is only flattery in disguise.

SANDFORD.

The captain is a courtier, quite a master of conver-
sational *finesse*.

LORD MERLIN.

Take care, Bob, what you say to the captain, or he'll pop you down in his "Life and Times."

EMILY MANIFOLD.

I don't think he *is* a courtier, Mr. Sandford. I was at Court on Wednesday, and I'm sure I never saw such a set. As to the lords, I wondered at them, they looked so mean and paltry; with red foxy faces and shrivelled bodies. There wasn't a lord amongst them had half such a figure as Captain Montague.

LADY MANIFOLD.

Oh!—my love, you forget there's a lord present. I'm afraid you'll make his lordship jealous of Captain Montague.

LORD MERLIN.

Don't be uneasy, madam. I will endeavour to endure the captain's muscles with philosophical resignation. Is that another member of your ladyship's family?

(*Looking towards* MABEL, *who still remains behind.*)

LADY MANIFOLD (*embarrassed*).

No—no—merely a dependant—an humble companion of my daughter's.

LORD MERLIN (*aside*).

The humble companion fairly eclipses the daughter. (*To* LADY MANIFOLD.) A *protégé*, eh?

LADY MANIFOLD.

Why—yes—the girl is an orphan, and Emily is so very generous.

SANDFORD (*who has been observing the scene with great anxiety, aside*).

I tremble with apprehension—I wonder what he thinks of Mabel.

LORD MERLIN.

She's a charming person. These " humble companions," your ladyship, are sometimes very interesting people. Do me the favour to make me known to the young lady.

LADY MANIFOLD.

Oh! my lord—you do her too much honour. Young persons in her situation ought not to be made too much of.

LORD MERLIN.

I suspect, madam, there is not much danger of her being spoiled in that way here. Pray introduce me.

SANDFORD (*aside*).

Noble uncle! I'll introduce her myself. (*To* LORD MERLIN.) As her ladyship seems a little reluctant, uncle, to make you acquainted with Miss Trevor, allow me the honour.

LORD MERLIN.

What! Bob—are you acquainted with the lady?

SANDFORD.

What, uncle—do you think when *you* could distinguish her amongst such a crowd, that *I* should never have noticed her before? (*To* LADY MANIFOLD.) With your permission, madam—(*To* MABEL)—Miss Trevor—*drawing her forward*)—This is my uncle, Lord Merlin—he is anxious for a special introduction to you, and—I hope you will pardon so great a liberty—I could not resist the happiness of gratifying him.

LORD MERLIN.

Of course, miss, you don't mind one word these young fellows say—especially my nephew. He's a feather, and dances along just as the wind blows.

SANDFORD (*aside*).

There's gratitude. He'll ruin me with Mabel for ever.

LORD MERLIN.

But I must not forget that I am indebted to him for the pleasure of this introduction.

MABEL TREVOR.

Your lordship confers much honour on me.

LORD MERLIN.

The honour and pleasure are conferred on me, Miss Trevor. (*Aside*) Her ladyship's fear of making too much of her, is quite intelligible—she's perfectly lovely.

LADY MANIFOLD (*interposing*).

Upon my word, gentlemen, you will set the poor child's head whirling. She so rarely hears such fine compliments, that I'm afraid you'll make her quite forget herself.

MABEL TREVOR.

Oh! madam, there is no danger of that.

LADY MANIFOLD (*aside to* MABEL).

Be silent—you are pert! (*Aloud*) Gentlemen, dancing has begun. Sir Gregory—you'll find cards in the next room. I know you dearly love a rubber.

SIR GREGORY PLUMP.

Your ladyship is very obliging—If your ladyship danced, I should certainly beg your hand—perhaps—

LADY MANIFOLD.

Whist I abhor.

LORD MERLIN.

Can't you get up a partnership on any score, Gregory?—not even for life? Her ladyship, who hates whist so heartily, must have a double horror of dumby.

LADY MANIFOLD.

Your lordship's brilliant spirits will put Sir Gregory out of humour with fortune, and should the luck run against him, he'll set it all down to me. But I'll come, Sir Gregory, and peep into your hand presently—

LORD MERLIN.

And you shall see there—

LADY MANIFOLD.

What in the name of wonder ?—

LORD MERLIN.

Only his heart, madam.   [SIR GREGORY *goes off*.

LADY MANIFOLD (*aside to* EMILY).

Positively, my dear, his lordship's the youngest man in the company. Now, my lord, will you give your arm to my daughter. Montague, yours—

LORD MERLIN.

But Miss Trevor—

LADY MANIFOLD (*with derision*).

Oh! Miss Trevor will find her way, by and by.

[*Exeunt* LADY MANIFOLD, CAPTAIN MONTAGUE, EMILY MANIFOLD, *and* LORD MERLIN; MABEL TREVOR *looks after them for a moment, then retires to a chair at the side.* SANDFORD *stands apart, observing her.*

SANDFORD.

Insolent and cruel. She struggles against it proudly, but it is too much for her gentle nature—I cannot bear it. (*He approaches and addresses her*) Miss Trevor, I fear you will blame my zeal, or indiscretion, for much of the pain Lady Manifold's oppressive treatment—

MABEL TREVOR.

Sir?

SANDFORD.

I beg pardon. I am conscious of meaning well, but, for my life, I cannot find the right way to express myself without risking your displeasure, and I would rather incur any penalty than that.

MABEL TREVOR.

You are very good, Mr. Sandford; but you must not pay me any compliments. You heard her ladyship say that they might make me forget myself. (*Half aside*) She little knows how much truth there was in her words.

SANDFORD.

Her ladyship is a mass of selfish vanity. She is jealous of your beauty and accomplishments, on account of her senseless daughter, and makes your position a pretext for loading you with injustice. I have observed it, and—and —in short, Miss Trevor, it ought to be resented.

MABEL TREVOR.

Resented, Mr. Sandford! Whatever my situation may be in this house, it does not warrant you in treating my feelings with disrespect.

SANDFORD (*with energy*).

You misunderstand me.

MABEL TREVOR (*hurriedly*).

No—no—I am sure your intention was kind; but perhaps we are proud in proportion as we are defenceless. Do not let me detain you from the ball-room. (*Moving up the stage.*)

SANDFORD.

You must not leave me thus. I am afraid you think me the wild, capricious fellow my uncle has described. I have faults enough, Heaven knows! but insincerity, at least, is not one of them. If I have offended you by presuming to express an interest in your happiness—

MABEL TREVOR.

Indeed, I am not offended, I am grateful; but, Mr. Sandford, this pains me—I—

SANDFORD.

You wrong yourself and me. Why should I struggle any longer to suppress the feelings you have inspired. They must have utterance or they will destroy me.

MABEL (*breathlessly while he is speaking*).

Ah!—spare me—I entreat—

SANDFORD.

Before I met you my thoughts were as free as birds, my feet were winged, I lived like air, as liberal and volatile. But from day to day, as I came here and saw you, I felt a change pass over my spirit. For the first time in my life, I grew sad and began to think solitude pleasant. What was that change, Mabel? The spell is broken! I have dared to speak aloud a name, which I have hitherto hardly trusted myself to breathe in whispers to my heart. Mabel, what was that change? 'Twas love.

MABEL (*who has been violently agitated throughout, sinks into a chair*).

Oh! Heaven.

SANDFORD (*after a pause*).

What does this silence mean? She turns from me—she loves another.

MABEL (*in a low broken voice*).

Recall what you have said—let it be forgotten at both sides—for your sake, Mr. Sandford—recall it—recall it—

SANDFORD.

For my sake? Then your affections are already—

MABEL TREVOR (*starting up*).

Oh!—no—not that.

SANDFORD.

Why do you turn from me, Mabel? In charity, relieve me from this terrible suspense—one word!

MABEL TREVOR.

What should that word be? I appeal to your own reason. Do not think me insensible of the honour you design me; but think of your circumstances and of mine. Think—think, Mr. Sandford, and answer for me what should that word be?

SANDFORD.

Circumstances? Oh! we must put all such considerations out of the question.

MABEL TREVOR.

I dare not. The happiness of a life-long home is not to be so lightly risked. I am an orphan—friendless—

E

alone, alone in this great wilderness of wealth and pomp:
—You are the happy heir of rich domains, with proud titles
in your blood, and high hopes dancing wild upon your
crest.   There is no alliance, however lofty, to which you
might not justly aspire.—A noble fortune lies before you,
and woos you to fame and honour.   Are you not answered ?

SANDFORD.

No, eloquent sophist !   You only make me love you the
more—you only give me fresh reasons for admiration of
your character.

MABEL TREVOR.

You see through a flattering medium.   What would be
said by your friends—I have none !—if this were known ?
No—no—not for the world would I endanger your peace,
your security.   Go forth into that bright circle, for which
nature has given you so many brilliant qualifications, and
leave me in the humility in which you found me.

SANDFORD.

Mabel—Mabel—you will distract me.   I see the effort
you are making—the heroic effort.   You tremble, and your
colour flies—it cannot be that I am indifferent to you.

MABEL (*with a great effort to rally*).

It is natural I should be slightly moved by so unex-
pected a declaration.   You suddenly flutter the still
monotony of my life, and expect me to be quite calm—
when you are gone, my serenity will return.

SANDFORD.

Never—your soul is touched with an enduring sympathy, and its tranquillity is fled for ever.   Revoke your

hard sentence, sweet Mabel, and lift me from despair (*throwing himself on his knees before her*).

MABEL TREVOR.

Is this generous?—Reflect upon our situation—where we are—

SANDFORD.

Let them come. The world is nothing to me without you—

MABEL TREVOR.

My heart will burst! my respiration is stifled—but I must be strong. Mr. Sandford—this must not be—we are not equals—under happier auspices, I might have listened —but as it is—no more! I am without friends, without fortune—I never felt the want of it till now!

SANDFORD (*grasping her hand*).

Tears! and I have drawn tears from your eyes, Mabel; and you tell me you do not love me?

MABEL (*energetically*).

I never said I did not love you—(*checking herself*)—I mean—(*bursts into tears, and hides her face in her hands*)— God help me!

SANDFORD.

Pardon, dear Mabel. I understand this strong emotion —I am so proud and happy, and yet so miserable—I feel as if tears were gushing from my eyes as they are raining fast from yours—this deep joy is so close to grief.

MABEL TREVOR.

I can scarcely articulate—all this is so strange—yet I might have guessed it!—and I did—I knew it—long since —long before you knew it! But it is over now—you have

betrayed me into the confession of a feeling which I thought
would have gone with me in silence to the grave.

SANDFORD.

A life of devotion shall repay you, my own Mabel, for
that delightful confession.   Hush! the dancers are coming
this way—let us not mingle with the noisy rioters.

    [*They retire to the side.   Groups form from the back.   A*
       dance; LORD MERLIN, LADY MANIFOLD, EMILY
       MANIFOLD, &c., *variously disposed.*

END OF ACT II.

ACT III.

SCENE I.

LORD MERLIN'S. *Breakfast-table in the centre.* SAND-
FORD *on a sofa at the side, with a table before him covered
with books, newspapers, letters, &c.*

SANDFORD (*reading a newspaper*).

" How it happened could not be accurately ascertained;
but the jury were unanimously of opinion that the unhappy
youth came by his death through what is commonly called
'Spontaneous Combustion.'" (*Strikes the newspaper with
his hand, crushes it up, and thrusts it under his head*) I
haven't slept a wink all night.   Strange, that I, who have
been knocking about for the last three years in all sorts of
London life, should be so completely *renversé* by a pair of
blue eyes.   Mabel, my own!   That's what has ruined me.
My own!   I never had any thing so precious belonging to
me before!   (*Rings a small bell on the table.*)   Loop.
(*Enter* LOOP.)   What o'clock is it?

LOOP.

Half-past eleven.

SANDFORD.

And my uncle not down yet. He's getting dissipated.
Go. (*Exit* LOOP.) Shall I tell him all about it? I ought
—I'm half afraid—he can be very severe when he has a
mind.   What am I to do?

   [*Rings the bell again with vehemence, but unconsciously.
   Enter* LOOP, *who stands waiting.* SANDFORD, *for-
   getting that he has rung the bell, hums a tune.*

LOOP.

Sir !

SANDFORD.

Well ?

LOOP.

Sir !

SANDFORD.

What do you want ?

LOOP.

Sir !

SANDFORD.

Go.

LOOP (aside).

Very odd !   Mr. Sandford's a—hem !   [*Exit.*

SANDFORD.

I daren't marry without his consent.   He'd cut me out of
every shilling.   It's not that exactly neither.   I owe the old
fellow gratitude.   He has always been so generous.   Here
he is !

Enter LORD MERLIN, *in a morning dress, leaning on*
BLOUNT.

LORD MERLIN (entering).

Blount, you're made of cast-iron.   You're just the same
man in the morning you are at night.   Are you there, Bob ?
I require an hour or two to settle down.   My head's never
exactly right in the morning.   Now, you have got such
damned inflexible nerves that you're fit for any thing the
moment you open your eyes.

BLOUNT.

So would you, if you went to bed at proper hours.

LORD MERLIN.

Grumble, grumble !   Tea !   (BLOUNT *rings the bell.
Servant enters with urn, &c., followed by* LOOP.)   Your voice

is as gruff as a bassoon. I never see you that I don't feel an instinct to stop my ears.

BLOUNT.

It would be wiser to keep them open.

LORD MERLIN.

Why, Surly?

BLOUNT.

Because you'd be sure to hear a little truth.

LORD MERLIN.

If you weren't as honest as the sun, Blount, I'd discharge you on the spot.

BLOUNT.

So you ought.

LORD MERLIN (*to* LOOP).

Put my letters in the next room. (*Exit* LOOP.) Blount, I'll ring for you when I want you. (*Exit* BLOUNT.) That fellow has a crust on him, like old wine—but he's sound and mellow at heart. Now, Bob, we'll have a quiet breakfast. Why, you look very pale! Any thing the matter?

SANDFORD.

Pale? Do I?—oh! I've been up these three hours—waiting for breakfast—as hungry as a hunter—

LORD MERLIN.

Well—(*they sit at table*)—that's soon remedied. Now you do the honours—I'm nothing till I get a cup of tea. That preposterous woman is running in my head still—why, Bob, you're pouring the tea into the sugar-basin!

SANDFORD.

Bless me, so I am! (*Rings the bell—enter* TOM.) Sugar.

LORD MERLIN.

That Miss—Miss Trevor—charming little gipsy.

SANDFORD.

You really think so ?—Water ! (*Enter* TOM *with sugar-basin, which he hands to* SANDFORD, *and exit.*) I'm over-joyed to hear you say so. (*Pours the sugar into the tea-pot.*)

LORD MERLIN.

Why, damn it, Bob, you're pouring the sugar into the teapot !

SANDFORD.

So I am ! (*Pushing away his cup and sitting a little apart.*)

LORD MERLIN (*after observing him in silence for a moment*).

Your appetite has vanished very quickly, Bob. I thought you were as hungry as a hunter !

SANDFORD.

My dear uncle, I beg your pardon—so I am—I had quite forgotten that I was so hungry. (*Turns to the table, and affects to eat with avidity.*)

LORD MERLIN.

Don't choke yourself—you can't deceive me—your pale looks—loss of appetite—you have thought proper, sir, to fall in love without consulting me—

SANDFORD.

I—I—(*stammering.*)

LORD MERLIN.

Well ?

SANDFORD.

Oh !—fall in love !—you speak so seriously—

LORD MERLIN.

Then, I suppose, it's merely a joke—perhaps you are only seducing the affections of some thoughtless girl, to deceive and desert her ?

SANDFORD.

Uncle, you do not think me capable of such baseness!

LORD MERLIN.

I don't think any thing about. You have no business to fall in love, in jest or earnest, without consulting me. Hark ye, young gentleman; if I had not conceived hopes of you, that you would keep yourself clear of all such stuff, and cultivate your talents for public life, I should never have adopted you. Take care what foolish attachments you form. I'll have no moonlight adventures—no underhand raptures. When you marry, you must look to rank, fortune, influence, or you shall have no countenance from me. But you've time enough to think of marriage these ten years.

SANDFORD.

That's all very true, uncle; yet there is such a thing in the world as real love—I mean—

LORD MERLIN.

You don't know what you mean. I'll tell you a story. I knew a youth who was just as inflammable as yourself—he had the same sort of enthusiasm—the same blind faith in the integrity of early passion! The only excuse I can make for him is that he was young like yourself, and ignorant of the world. Well—the fool!—he fell in love, as it is called; and certainly no man ever had a fairer prospect of happiness. The lady was young, had great expectations and unparalleled beauty. She pledged herself to him by every sacred promise. It went on for a year, for two years—such heaps of letters as passed between them!—one hardly knows how such things are brought about, but they do happen, and one gets over the agony somehow, harrowing as it is at the time. She was perfidious to him!—even while she continued to write to him, her woman's soul, fickle, vain, and easily forsworn, was vibrating and hesitating. She made an excuse to go into the country— the next time he heard of her, she was married! Do you wonder, after this, that I should distrust love-matches?— that I should warn you, through whom I hope to transmit a solid inheritance, against being duped and blighted by a romantic reliance upon the steadfastness of a woman?

SANDFORD.

But, my dear uncle, all women are not so false.

LORD MERLIN.

Every man thinks himself exempt from the common fate—I thought so—I used to laugh at such stories—I thought myself as secure—

SANDFORD.

You?—then you—

LORD MERLIN.

Yes. I am ashamed to be betrayed into the admission: but if it warn you against a similar misery, I shan't repent the passing anguish of a recollection long buried in a life of solitude! [*Exit.*

SANDFORD.

My poor uncle! Of all men—that he should be blasted at the very root. He would no more consent to a marriage with Mabel—an orphan, without a penny, without connexions— oh! the thing's hopeless—hopeless—hopeless! I shall go distracted. It would be easy enough to disobey my uncle —nothing easier!—if I could work myself up into a fit of heartless ingratitude. But suppose I did—what then? Draw poor Mabel into a life of penury—without one farthing of income from any source whatever, or the means of creating it. I wish they had made me a shoemaker—any thing rather than a gentleman. I'm fit for nothing. I know nothing—I can learn nothing. I'm conscious only of loving Mabel, and of being tolerably certain that I shall act like a—— my head's turning round like a top. What's to become of me? I must think—think— [*Exit.*

Enter LOOP *showing in* SIR GREGORY PLUMP.

SIR GREGORY PLUMP.

You told me his lordship was at breakfast?

LOOP.

Well, they have made uncommon haste, Sir Gregory. I suppose my lord's dressing. I beg your pardon, Sir Gregory, but as you have stood a contested election, perhaps you can tell me whether a quarterly tenant has a right to vote for the County of Middlesex?

SIR GREGORY PLUMP.

Why do you ask?

LOOP.

Why, the truth is, I have a little box in the country—I don't reside there exactly, only by deputy you understand—and, in short, I have been solicited for my vote.

SIR GREGORY PLUMP.

You have? I'll consult his lordship—I hear him on the stairs.

LOOP.

Oh! by no means, Sir Gregory—I—(*aside*)—If I had fifty votes *he* shouldn't have one of them.   [*Exit.*

Enter LORD MERLIN.

SIR GREGORY PLUMP.

Ha! ha! ha! Do you know, my lord, that your fellow here has a box in the country, and wants to know whether he can vote at elections.

LORD MERLIN.

Was he afraid you'd beg it of him, Gregory, that he wouldn't wait to be polled? (*Looking round.*) Is Sandford gone? H——m! (*Walks up and down thoughtfully.*) Do you know, Gregory, I've a great mind to go abroad.

SIR GREGORY PLUMP.

What, tired of the gay world so soon?

LORD MERLIN.

Sick of it. My head aches after last night. On cool reflection there's no pleasure in a miscellaneous gathering of people who never saw each other before, and who don't care if they never see each other again. It's a grand mistake to call it enjoyment.

SIR GREGORY PLUMP.

You'll make me think you capricious. Why, last night you were the very soul of hilarity—I never saw a man in such high spirits. Your conversation was a perpetual shower of arrowy jokes; you stopped at nothing; you danced, sang, and, between ourselves, quite bewildered the pretty little girl in white.

LORD MERLIN.

No!—Did I? (*chuckling.*) She's a love, Gregory; I never saw such a hand—such a foot—such a mouth!

SIR GREGORY PLUMP.

Yet, you talk of giving up the gay world?

LORD MERLIN.

So I do—I talk of it.

SIR GREGORY PLUMP.

Pshaw! it's only in the mornings you are philosophical—at night you'll be carried away again :—six hours of pleasure—twelve of sleep—and six of headach, repentance, and the toilet.

LORD MERLIN.

You're mistaken. I've had enough of it. I'll go abroad, or lock myself up again in my club.

SIR GREGORY PLUMP.

And leave your nephew to be ruined by late hours and contraband amours.

LORD MERLIN.

He'll be ruined in spite of me. You know what I've done for that fellow : well, sir, he has the ingratitude to look as pale as a ghost, and to sit down to breakfast without a particle of appetite. I'm firmly resolved never to—(*Enter* TOM *with a card, which he hands to* LORD MERLIN). Look here!

SIR GREGORY PLUMP (*reading the card*).

"Captain Swinford Hastings Montague." What can be object of his visit?

LORD MERLIN.

An ambassador with secret instructions from Lady Manifold. Show the gentleman up.   [*Exit* TOM.

SIR GREGORY PLUMP.

Let us indulge the egotist, and we may get some useful hints.

Enter CAPTAIN MONTAGUE.

MONTAGUE.

My lord—happy to have the honour !—Sir Gregory, how d'ye do ?—'pon my life, a superb mansion this !

LORD MERLIN.

Pretty well, sir—pretty well.

MONTAGUE.

I know it's rude to notice things, but—'pon my life, this house is something peculiar.

SIR GREGORY PLUMP.

You seem to be a good judge of interiors, captain ?

MONTAGUE.

I fancy I have rather a genius that way. What an admirable room for a select dinner (*walking across the stage*). You could dine twenty here luxuriously. I don't know whether your lordship entertains. Are you celebrated for your dinners ?

LORD MERLIN.

Not that I'm aware of.

MONTAGUE.

M—m ! I called on your lordship about a little confidential business—(*looking significantly towards* SIR GREGORY).

LORD MERLIN.

My friend, Sir Gregory, is in my confidence in every thing.

MONTAGUE.

Sir Gregory is a man of honour—(*crossing over, and shaking hands in the centre with* SIR GREGORY)—I am proud, Sir Gregory, to shake such a friend by the hand.

The truth is, I have rather a singular communication to make—but—you pledge yourselves?

SIR GREGORY PLUMP.

Oh! certainly—sacred!

MONTAGUE.

I dare say you think me rather an unsettled sort of fellow. You're mistaken. I'm an observer of character. I think I told you I was writing my " Life and Times"—so I did! My father was a gentleman—limited estate—bee-hives—gold and silver fish—every thing elegant—on a small scale—Lancashire. He was a seventh son—I'm another. Couldn't be expected that the seventh son of a seventh son—seven times seven, forty-nine!—should inherit much property. I inherited none. My grandfather bought me a commission. I'm on half-pay.

SIR GREGORY PLUMP.

And you have managed to live on your half-pay.

MONTAGUE.

What I've managed *not* to do is still more extraordinary. I have not got into debt. Wonderful?

SIR GREGORY PLUMP.

Very. How did you manage that?

MONTAGUE.

Can't tell—don't know myself. It surprises you? *You* can't understand how a man can dress well—(*showing his coat*)—Bond-street—and keep himself in decent society on three-and-fourpence a day. I'm used to it.

SIR GREGORY PLUMP.

And nothing else? No property of any kind?

MONTAGUE.

Yes—I forgot.   I have 150,000 acres of uncleared land
—Central America.

SIR GREGORY PLUMP.

Actual acres ?

MONTAGUE.

No—Scrip!   They couldn't get any body to buy it;
made it a present to me.   Temperate climate—vegetation
of the tropics—rising country—sell it cheap !

LORD MERLIN.

And so, without begging, borrowing, or stealing, you
contrive to exist, and to wear Bond-street coats, on three-
and-fourpence a day.   You're a greater hero, captain, than
Marlborough or Wellington.

MONTAGUE.

It requires some little management, though.   I don't
show the whole year round.   I'm out only in the height of
the season.   The rest of the year I'm laid up, like a ship
in commission ; or, as they say on the turf, I'm nowhere.

LORD MERLIN.

But you mentioned that you had a communication to
make—

MONTAGUE.

No doubt you think it odd I should let you into my
private history.   Not at all.   I wish you to know me.   In
fact, it's necessary you should know me thoroughly, or we
can't pull together.

LORD MERLIN.

Pull together !

MONTAGUE.

Lady Manifold requested me to call on your lordship.
" You can just drop a hint carelessly in the course of con-

versation," said her ladyship, "that my daughter is very anxious to have his lordship's opinion of a horse—he's such a judge of horses."

LORD MERLIN.

I never bought a horse on my own judgment in my life !

MONTAGUE.

" But on no account," said her ladyship, "let it appear that I sent such a message to him. It can't be helped, you know," said she, laughing in her own irresistible way, Sir Gregory, "if his lordship should find out that my daughter is over head and ears in love with him; but I wouldn't for the world his lordship should imagine I wished him to know it !"

LORD MERLIN.

What do you think of that, Gregory ?

SIR GREGORY PLUMP.

That it's the most formidable nibble I ever heard of.

MONTAGUE.

I thought you'd like to know exactly what she said.

LORD MERLIN.

To be frank with you, captain, I didn't much fancy you at first. But I see you're an honest, incomprehensible fellow.

MONTAGUE.

'Pon my life, I'm very proud of your acquaintance. Dine at seven? I shall be punctual. I'll give you a proof of my confidence. Her ladyship is trying to draw you into a marriage with Miss Manifold.

LORD MERLIN.

I guessed as much.

MONTAGUE.

Now, I must put your confidence to the test. You must know—honour!—that Miss Manifold and I are privately bespoke—devotedly attached. You're astonished? I'll make a first-rate husband.

LORD MERLIN (*half-aside*).

Quite good enough for her.

MONTAGUE.

I have no vices—a few faults.

SIR GREGORY PLUMP.

The partition is so thin, captain, that it's hardly worth while to make an invidious distinction between them.

MONTAGUE.

The best thing I've heard you say, Sir Gregory. I'll pop that into my " Life and Times." Let us return to our mutton. Miss Manifold put me in possession of her mother's schemes, one of which was that she, Miss Manifold, was to flirt with me—with me!—to make you jealous. Wasn't that capital? I mean to flirt to some purpose. I intend to run away with her. Biter bit, eh?

LORD MERLIN.

Bit with a vengeance.

MONTAGUE.

Under these pressing circumstances I throw myself upon your honour. Sorry to frustrate you—but, backed by the old lady, power, &c.—you're rather a dangerous rival.

LORD MERLIN.

Captain Montague, you have been so candid with me, that you're entitled to an explicit answer. Run away with the girl whenever you please, only don't ask me to be privy to your plans. I shall rejoice to hear that the calculations of the match-making mother are foiled; but I can't exactly join in a deception upon her.

MONTAGUE.

Spoken like a gentleman! I'll show you that I'm capable of an act of generosity. Sir Gregory, you're paying court to the widow. I know all about it. I *can* assist you, and I will.

SIR GREGORY PLUMP.

My dear sir, you are very—

MONTAGUE.

Don't mention it. It's not my interest she should marry, because Mrs. Montague that is to be, would naturally inherit her fortune. But I don't care about that. I should like you for a father-in-law. Won't we crack a bottle together when we're married!

SIR GREGORY PLUMP.

But how is it to be brought about, captain.

MONTAGUE.

I'll tell you. Enter into her confidence. Tell her that I have disclosed her manœuvres to his lordship, and that I'm going to run away with her daughter. Make a merit of it. Don't mind me—there'll be a storm—but I'll have a life-boat ready. She'll be so grateful to you for the discovery, that it will be your own fault if you don't succeed.

SIR GREGORY PLUMP.

But will it be honourable to betray you?

MONTAGUE.

To be sure it will, when it's with my own consent. I know Lady Manifold's weak side, and I believe, my lord, that it's a woman's weak side we generally find most vulnerable in love affairs.

LORD MERLIN.

Gregory, take the captain's advice. You can't be in abler hands. He knows the quarry well, and will show you how to hunt it down. I have letters to write, and must leave you. So good morning—(*aside*)—Bob not returned yet!
[*Exit.*

MONTAGUE.

Will you go with me to Lady Manifold's?

SIR GREGORY PLUMP.

With all my heart.

MONTAGUE.

What was that he said about a quarry? Tell me as we go along. I'll pop it into my " Life and Times." [*Exeunt.*

SCENE II.

LADY MANIFOLD'S. *A window at the back, opening upon a conservatory.* EMILY *seated in the conservatory.* LADY MANIFOLD *standing at the window.*

LADY MANIFOLD.

I tell you, my love, you don't understand it. His lordship's attentions to Mabel were quite remarkable. You know, my dear, I couldn't suffer such a scandal to go forward in my house.

EMILY MANIFOLD.

I'm sure I don't care what attentions he shows her.

LADY MANIFOLD (*coming forward*).

That's your simplicity. You have no business *not* to care about *any thing* his lordship does. Mercy, love! what will become of you when you're married if you don't know when to care, and when not to care.

EMILY MANIFOLD.

I suppose I'll learn as you did.

LADY MANIFOLD.

Then the sooner you begin the better. I tell you that his lordship was most marked in his attentions to Mabel.

EMILY MANIFOLD.

And I tell you I don't care whether he was or not.

LADY MANIFOLD.

But I tell you, you ought to care.

EMILY MANIFOLD.

But I tell you I can't care. I'm trying to care as fast as I can, but I can't.

LADY MANIFOLD (*aside*).

She hasn't the least notion of being jealous. I'll make another experiment. (*To* EMILY) Emily, love,—look at me, dear, and put away that stupid book; you're not reading now, you know. Emily, I'll send Mabel out of the house.

EMILY MANIFOLD.

Well, you may if you like, but I don't see the good of it.

LADY MANIFOLD.

It will prevent Lord Merlin from having any opportunity of seeing her.

EMILY MANIFOLD.

I think, ma, it will *give* him opportunity of seeing her.

LADY MANIFOLD.

How, my innocent?

EMILY MANIFOLD.

Because if he wants to see her, he can follow her wherever she goes, and you can't prevent him; but if you keep her in the house, she can't see him without your permission.

LADY MANIFOLD.

That's very true. I'll forbid her to see him.

EMILY MANIFOLD.

I'm sure, ma, I wouldn't.

LADY MANIFOLD.

Why, love?

EMILY MANIFOLD.

Because it will make her think too much of him. I'm sure if any one were to say to me that I shouldn't see Captain—(*checking herself*)—any one, I'd never be happy till I saw them.

LADY MANIFOLD (*aside*).

What an union of sagacity and guilelessness! (*To* EMILY) Well, love, I'll take your advice (*ringing the bell*).

I'll only just tell her that she must not—(*Enter* Servant)—desire Miss Trevor to come here—(*Exit* Servant)—that she must not make herself too prominent
when we have company.

Enter Mabel.

MABEL TREVOR.

You wished to see me, madam.

LADY MANIFOLD.

Yes, Mabel, I wished to say a few words to you about
your manners in public.

MABEL TREVOR.

Madam !

LADY MANIFOLD.

You know, Mabel, that when I took you into my house—
I have no wish to hurt your feelings, and you must not let
your pride be in the way of your interest—you know the
situation it was understood you were to fill.

MABEL TREVOR.

I do, madam.   You were kind enough to say that,
knowing my family, you would not exact any menial
offices at my hands.

LADY MANIFOLD.

And have I ?

MABEL TREVOR.

Oh ! no, madam.   I have not been put to any menial
services.

LADY MANIFOLD.

But, you mean, you have been treated as a menial.

MABEL TREVOR.

I have not complained, madam.

LADY MANIFOLD.

Really, I have no desire to enter into an argument with you, Mabel; my object in sending for you was simply to remind you, that when I have company in this house, I expect you will not forget your position.   You talked and laughed so much with Lord Merlin—(EMILY *checks her*) and other gentlemen last night, that positively one might almost suppose you were my daughter's sister or cousin, instead of a dependant.

MABEL TREVOR.

Did I laugh and talk? Oh! madam, you have made some strange mistake.. But I beg pardon—I am a dependant—I may not always be one !

LADY MANIFOLD.

You are too proud, Mabel.   Your spirit is above your place.   You get up such a catalogue of grievances in your face, that a stranger might actually suppose you were treated with the coarsest cruelty.

MABEL TREVOR.

No, madam ; with the most refined.

LADY MANIFOLD.

" Pray reserve your smart answers for your inferiors, Miss Trevor.   I must beg that you will not forget yourself again while you are in my house.

MABEL TREVOR.

" Indeed, I try, madam, to do as you desire me—but you crush me with the weight of your protection.   Whatever I do is wrong—and then the distance between us—it chills me.

LADY MANIFOLD.

" Distance ! Perhaps you expect to be placed on a level with Miss Manifold, who has been brought up with such expense and care ? Distance !"* Let me hear no more such observations.

MABEL TREVOR.

I am silent, madam.

LADY MANIFOLD.

I wish you would learn to be silent before company. " What will Lord Merlin think of the decorum of my house, after last night ? I, who am so particular about the conduct of young people ?

MABEL TREVOR.

" Lord Merlin ? Decorum ? Last night ? You are bound, madam, in common justice to explain the calumny you point at me. Were I even humbler than I am, you ought not—you shall not whisper away my character.

LADY MANIFOLD.

" Character ? Who ever thought of your character ? I really didn't imagine such an idea ever entered your head. Mercy upon us ! but things are surely taking a strange turn, when our very pensioners must threaten us with their characters."*

Enter SERVANT.

SERVANT.

Sir Gregory Plump and Captain Montague are in the library, my lady, and they desired me to say that they have just come from Lord Merlin's.

---

* Omitted in the representation.

LADY MANIFOLD.

We shall be with them presently. (*Exit* SERVANT.)
Come, my love. I dare say his lordship will he here to
look at your horse. Miss Trevor, we shall not trouble you
to appear in the drawing-room this evening. Come, my
love. What a sweet colour you have, child !

[*Exit with* EMILY, *patting her on the cheek.*

MABEL TREVOR.

The insolence of power !—the abuse of rank and fortune !
I should sink under this, or die in the struggle to redeem
myself from it, but for the new life, and the new love of
life with which I am inspired. What a change a few hours
have made in my destiny ! I am no longer desolate, looking
out in despair upon a living world, in which nothing lives
for me. I am no longer alone. Thank God for that !
Robert—I love even the echo of his name. He—he will
protect me. I am strong in his strength—in his pure and
high, and ennobling love. He will protect me !—(*Enter*
SANDFORD, *hastily, with a disturbed air.*)—Ah ! I am so
glad to see you !

SANDFORD.

My dear Mabel !

MABEL TREVOR.

I was thinking of you at that moment.

SANDFORD.

Indeed ! and I—Mabel—I was thinking of you !

MABEL TREVOR.

Are you ill ?

SANDFORD.

Ill !—No—

MABEL TREVOR.

You are very pale.

SANDFORD.

So my uncle says—nothing !—I couldn't sleep last night !—but, Mabel, your hand trembles—has any thing happened ?

MABEL TREVOR.

Oh ! perhaps, I oughtn't to tell you.

SANDFORD.

I must know—concealments between us, Mabel, are dangerous.

MABEL TREVOR.

There shall be none.   Lady Manifold has just been reminding me that I am a dependant upon her bounty. She has hinted something about my laughing and talking last night—it seems I was in great spirits ! You can answer for the cause, if it were so !

SANDFORD.

Well ?

MABEL TREVOR.

Well !—it hurt me—wounded me, that I should be accused of levity—that's all. But then I remembered that I was no longer unprotected ! and I thought how proudly you would vindicate me, and—(*perceiving gradually that he has turned from her, she drops her voice.*) You *are* ill ?

SANDFORD (*shuddering*).

No—no—upon my honour !

MABEL TREVOR.

Honour ! What is the matter ?—Tell me—I have a

right to know—a right to—right?   My heart dies in the
word—that I should have need to use it!

SANDFORD.

Come—come, Mabel; you are agitated.   Perhaps you
misunderstood her ladyship.

MABEL TREVOR.

Is it possible?   That you, who only last night were so
full of indignation at her cruelty, which I have borne so
long without a murmur, should tell me, now that she has
added insult to oppression, that I have misunderstood her!

SANDFORD.

Mabel, for Heaven's sake, be calm.

MABEL TREVOR.

Calm?   I am—I am—I am stone.

SANDFORD.

What is this?   What have I said?   Wretched, wretched
Sandford.

MABEL TREVOR.

Wretched, indeed, if you repent what you have done.

SANDFORD.

Repent—no—I love you with my whole being.

MABEL TREVOR.

You do not.   If you did, and heard that I had been
wronged, or that but a breath of slander, however distant,
however faint, had fallen upon me, you would have answered it with a look of lightning.   You do not love me!

SANDFORD.

Oh! Mabel, if you knew the tortures I suffer—recollect
your own words—the circumstances you described—

MABEL TREVOR.

I see it now. The truth breaks upon me.

SANDFORD.

To what horrid issue will this lead?

MABEL TREVOR.

You have reconsidered:—why hesitate? Take courage, speak. I am again defenceless!

SANDFORD.

No—no— I will protect you. Why should conventional laws restrain our love?

MABEL TREVOR.

Have my senses forsook their office? Speak again.

SANDFORD.

Mabel, hear me! Like yourself, I am a dependant. I have no fortune of my own. My whole expectations hang upon my uncle. With one word he could consign me to destitution.

MABEL TREVOR.

You must not offend your uncle.

SANDFORD.

I dare not—he was kind to me when I had no other friend in the world. But he has different notions of marriage—of high connexions—fortune—there is my misery. If we could conceal our attachment from him, we might be happy—

MABEL TREVOR.

Conceal? It is ended for ever—what have we to conceal?

SANDFORD.

You must not speak thus.   I will never marry.   He will be content with that.   I'm sure he will.   I will devote my life to you, Mabel—(*Rushes forward to take her hand.*)

MABEL TREVOR.

Do not touch me.   My hand shrinks from you, as my soul does.   Had you the wealth of England, and its noblest titles, and poured them out at my feet, I would scorn them, as I scorn you now!   Oh! how I have been deceived. 'Tis over.   I explained to you my situation—I warned you against the inequality of our circumstances—you overruled my feeble reason—you wrung from me the secret of my woman's heart.   You have broken that heart! a heart that loved and trusted you.   I cannot disguise the bitterness of this trial. But even at this moment of agony, that broken heart, in the depth of its purity, revolts from you.   Begone!   We never, never meet again.   [*Exit.*

SANDFORD.

Villain—villain! where shall I hide my disgrace.

[*Rushes out.*

END OF ACT III.

ACT IV.

SCENE I.

ROSE's *room at* LADY MANIFOLD's. *Engravings hung on the walls — circulating library books on shelves — a cast of Cupid stands amongst them.* ROSE *seated, spreading out a pack of cards on a small table at the side.*

ROSE.

Shuffle and cut !—do what I will, she always comes up— That's money—and a ring !—Well, I never—He's talking to the knave of diamonds—and it's about a house, and— another dark woman !—Oh ! the Turk—such a drab—no, that's me—now for it. Heigho ! There's my sooty rival again. I'll shut her up, the toad ! and cut for a wish. Now what shall I wish for ? Wish to have a fine house and two lovers and plenty of money.

Enter LOOP.
LOOP (*after observing her*).

Positively, child, you are telling fortunes.

ROSE.

Mr. Loop !—You make me vibrate !

LOOP (*not heeding her*).

You haven't got such a thing as a thought of silk, have you?
ROSE (*takes a threadcase out of her pocket*).

LOOP.

Just tie my bouquet.

ROSE (*dallying with the flowers in his buttonhole, and looking up in his face*).

I'm all of a twitter—he!—he!—oh! lauk, you're getting so thin—

LOOP.

Am I? So much the better. It's monstrous vulgar to be fat. I keep myself down by a narrow regimen and vinegar.

ROSE (*turning away and pouting*).

Then it isn't love does it.

LOOP (*surveying himself in the glass*).

Love? what's that?

ROSE.

Why the man's quite altered. You're a bear? Where are your raptures when you came in? Why don't you rush—

LOOP.

Hush! Love must be enjoyed with the greatest economy. Diet yourself sparingly, or you risk a surfeit. Love never dies of short commons, but frequently of indigestion.*

ROSE.

You've cooled down since Sunday last. Didn't you say to me, " It's an eternity since I saw you!" What did you mean by an eternity?

LOOP.

Two days.

ROSE.

I see it! The dark young woman, the ring! you're going to be married.

---

* Ninon de L'Enclos sets up a similar theory in one of her famous letters to the Marquis de Sévigné.

LOOP.

If I marry it must be a fortune. Would you like to be Mrs. Loop, child?

ROSE.

Oh! fie, Mr. Loop. What a question!

LOOP.

But I had almost forgotten what brought me here, Rose.

ROSE.

Don't Rose me.

LOOP.

You can keep a secret?

ROSE.

Try me.

LOOP.

I've got a letter in my pocket.

ROSE.

For me?

LOOP.

No—for Miss Trevor.

ROSE (*in a burst of indignation*).

You're not a corresponding with *her*?

LOOP.

I'm not such a ninny. The letter's a dead secret. You're to deliver it. Here's half-a-sovereign from Mr. Sandford—for your trouble. (*Aside*) The other half I'll keep myself.

ROSE.

Is it a love-letter?

LOOP.

Confidentially, I suspect it is.

G

ROSE.

And you pollute it with lucre. Take back the gold.

LOOP.

With the greatest pleasure.

ROSE.

She looks it. She has such a way with her lips—always biting them ! And Mr. Sandford's the man.

LOOP.

Sandford's a dolt. I can't make head or tail of him. Marriage is out of the question, you know. The girl hasn't as much coin as would turn the empty scale of a post-office balance.

ROSE.

And do you think there's any thing wrong between them ?

LOOP.

Can't say, really. I suppose something has happened, for he was like a rag in a high wind this morning. But the letter's a settler, I fancy. Observe, you're to insist upon her taking it, whether she likes it or not.

ROSE.

Dear me, I wonder what's in it ! (*trying to peep into it.*) What a sly thing she is ! Why, she looks as demure as a post, and may be, for all we know, she is——I declare, there she is coming down the stairs. Don't let her see you in my room, or she'll think I'm as bad as herself.

LOOP.

Insist upon her taking it.

ROSE.

Go, deceiver, go!

LOOP.

You must positively sup with me some night in my country box. Good-by, child. (*Aside*) Rose is a victim.—Good-by—adieu!—   [*Exit·*

ROSE.

Sup with him—and that's all. I'm a living warning to all young maidens, how they give up their juvenile affections.   [*Exit.*

SCENE II.

Drawing-room at LADY MANIFOLD's. *Enter* LADY MANIFOLD *at the back, followed by* SIR GREGORY PLUMP.

LADY MANIFOLD.

Your declaration astonishes me, Sir Gregory. I'm not offended, but at my time of life—although I'm not exactly old—such subjects are generally treated historically.

SIR GREGORY PLUMP.

At your time of life, your ladyship, they are generally treated with the seriousness they deserve. Younger people may affect transports—we understand them.

LADY MANIFOLD.

Well, how that may be, I won't venture to say:—but such a serious question requires time—

SIR GREGORY PLUMP.

Which neither of us have to spare. Now, just consider Lady Manifold your situation and mine. What are we living for? The world? The world does not care a pinch of snuff for us. It's all very well in company—but when we're alone! Think of that. We want a little comfort—somebody to tease, somebody to please, somebody to take the chill off our lives.

LADY MANIFOLD.

Don't you think, Sir Gregory, you have found out the necessity of taking the chill off, as you call it, rather late? Ten or fifteen years ago—

SIR GREGORY PLUMP.

Your husband was alive.

LADY MANIFOLD.

But there were a hundred ladies of your acquaintance who had no husband.

SIR GREGORY PLUMP.

Yes—but there was only one Lady Manifold.

LADY MANIFOLD.

Now, don't put on such a piece of affectation. You surely did not entertain any such foolish notions in poor Sir Richard's lifetime.

SIR GREGORY PLUMP.

Such notions might have been very foolish then—but you'll admit they are very rational now. Besides, impressions are fleeting in one's youth; but at my age they take deeper root. You wouldn't break my heart, would you?

LADY MANIFOLD.

Oh! not for the world. At your age I suspect hearts

are not so very easily broken. The difficulty is to know
how to get at them, old or young. Seriously—

SIR GREGORY PLUMP.

Well, seriously.

LADY MANIFOLD.

Well, seriously—ha ! ha ! ha ! I beg your pardon. I'm
highly complimented and all that. But—ha ! ha ! ha !

SIR GREGORY PLUMP.

But ?

LADY MANIFOLD.

But—but—

SIR GREGORY PLUMP.

I'll fill up the but—you won't marry till you've settled
your daughter.

LADY MANIFOLD.

Undoubtedly, that is one consideration.

SIR GREGORY PLUMP.

Now if I were her father-in-law, I might—Lord Merlin
is my intimate friend.

LADY MANIFOLD.

So he is.

SIR GREGORY PLUMP.

He takes an interest in her settlement, and mine too.

LADY MANIFOLD.

His lordship is very obliging.

SIR GREGORY PLUMP.

I am aware of your anxiety to make him your son-in-
law, and the plans you have laid for that purpose.

LADY MANIFOLD.

Plans, Sir Gregory ?

SIR GREGORY PLUMP.

Come, let us be confidential. You don't suppose I blame you for desiring so good a match for your daughter? Not at all.

LADY MANIFOLD.

But who told you this?

SIR GREGORY PLUMP.

Captain Montague. He told it to Lord Merlin also. It's no longer a secret.

LADY MANIFOLD.

You shock me! Montague's a viper.

SIR GREGORY PLUMP.

I have, certainly, no right to interfere; and if I didn't happen to be acquainted with other matters that are going forward, without your knowledge, respecting your daughter—

LADY MANIFOLD.

Other matters?

SIR GREGORY PLUMP.

I don't think I should have taken the liberty—

LADY MANIFOLD.

Liberty! my dear Sir Gregory, how can you use such a word—you've done me the greatest kindness—go on.

SIR GREGORY PLUMP.

Perhaps I ought not to go any farther. I am a mere friend like any body else, and family affairs are family affairs. But feeling towards your ladyship as I do, I confess, if I had any hope—

LADY MANIFOLD.

My dear Sir Gregory, I always had a sincere regard

for you—indeed, I might use a stronger term. The truth is, if my daughter were married, I don't hesitate to say I should be rather lonely; and as you were observing just now, one does want somebody to tease, and, in short, I think, if my daughter were married, I should have no great objection—

SIR GREGORY PLUMP.

To get married yourself. Let me kiss your hand upon it, and command me for life.

LADY MANIFOLD.

Well—there's my hand.

SIR GREGORY PLUMP (*kissing it*).

And seal.

LADY MANIFOLD.

One would think you were putting the family coat of arms on it by the pressure of the stamp. Now, my dear Sir Gregory, you will conceal nothing from me?

SIR GREGORY PLUMP.

Well, then, don't do any thing rash. Montague is in love with Emily.

LADY MANIFOLD.

Mon—Mon—in love—I'll choke!

SIR GREGORY PLUMP.

More than that—he intends to run away with her. (*Aside*) The murder's out.

LADY MANIFOLD.

Run away with her! A grub of a half-pay lieutenant run away with my daughter. I should have suspected him of running away with some of my silver spoons sooner. I'll have him transported.

SIR GREGORY PLUMP.

There—I was afraid you'd be hasty. We must act with
discretion.

LADY MANIFOLD.

There's no discretion in the case, Sir Gregory; my innocent child, that knows nothing of the world, to be tre-
panned into an elopement with an adventurer. To think
that she should be unconsciously standing on the edge of
such a precipice! Discretion, indeed!

SIR GREGORY PLUMP.

My dear madam, you must be calm. Lord Merlin
treats the business with contempt, and it is not wise in you
to take it up so seriously.

LADY MANIFOLD.

Perhaps you are right. To be sure, although it's very
provoking, people in our station ought not to be ruffled by
such earthworms.

SIR GREGORY PLUMP.

His lordship and Miss Manifold are coming this way.
Just laugh at it, good-humouredly.

LADY MANIFOLD.

Well—well. I'll carry it off as well as I can. (*Enter*
LORD MERLIN *and* EMILY.) My dear lord, I'm charmed
to see you. I hope Emily has been trying to amuse you.
What a flush you're in, love! His lordship has been
paying you one of his fine compliments—that's it!—Have
you been showing him your drawings? She has a wonderful talent that way, hasn't she? (*Aside to* EMILY) Say
that you never got a lesson.

EMILY MANIFOLD.

You know, ma, I never got a lesson.

LADY MANIFOLD.

Never, I declare. We were afraid it would spoil her genius. *Apropos*, you've heard all about Montague, and his designs upon Emily?

LORD MERLIN.

From his own lips.

LADY MANIFOLD.

Isn't it irresistibly ridiculous? One can't be too careful in admitting such people to one's house; but we had him only to amuse us, and thought no more of him than we should of a monkey or a parrot—did we, love? I'm sure neither my daughter nor myself ever dreamt of his falling in love! Such a thing could never have entered my head in a thousand years! Poor wretch—only think of his being in love with her! and actually having the audacity to scheme a runaway match.

LORD MERLIN.

His audacity is undeniable.

LADY MANIFOLD.

Of course, we must never admit him into the house again. Of course not. I couldn't bear to do any thing positively cruel to him; for after all, you know, he couldn't help admiring her; but we can never countenance him any more. If you should ever meet him by any accident, child, you'll know what to do.

EMILY MANIFOLD.

Yes, ma—I'll know what to do.

LADY MANIFOLD.

You may depend upon it, my lord, she'll teach him to run away with young ladies of family—won't you, love?

EMILY MANIFOLD.

That I will, ma!

LADY MANIFOLD.

Will you follow us, my lord, into the conservatory. Don't let us interrupt your *tête-à-tête.* I want you, Sir Gregory, to look at my orange-trees. (*Aside to* SIR GREGORY *as they go off*) Was that thrown off well ?

SIR GREGORY PLUMP.

It was perfect.

[*Exit* LADY MANIFOLD *and* SIR GREGORY.

LORD MERLIN.

You hear what your mother says about the captain?

EMILY MANIFOLD.

Yes, but I don't heed it. If she's so against my marrying him, why did she encourage him here so much.

LORD MERLIN.

There's a great deal of sound sense in that. Moral— Mothers who expose their daughters to indiscriminate associations must take the consequences.

[ROSE *peeps in at the side, with a bonnet and shawl in her hand.*

ROSE.

Miss Emily !—hist !—Miss Emily—

EMILY MANIFOLD.

Well, Rose— what's the matter ?

ROSE.

I beg pardon—I didn't know any one was here—I mustn't speak before his lordship.

EMILY MANIFOLD.

Oh! yes, you may. What is it?

ROSE.

There, miss, the captain is waiting for you in the square —he has put me into such a fidget!—there he is, walking up and down under the trees, and beating his boots with a whip, so that you'd think he cut them to pieces—he's in a furious hurry—so I brought your bonnet and shawl—don't lose a minute, miss—

EMILY MANIFOLD.

Oh! mercy—make haste—there—(*putting on the shawl flurriedly the wrong way*)— there's a spell upon the shawl, I do believe—where's my boa?—

ROSE.

Oh! don't mind the boa—

EMILY MANIFOLD.

My gloves?—

ROSE.

Oh! don't mind your gloves, miss—go as your are—if my lady should come—

EMILY MANIFOLD.

That will do, Rose—there—thank you—oh! dear how my heart beats—good-by, my lord—I'm sorry I can't stay to amuse your lordship—good-by!   [*Exit.*

ROSE.

Run—run, miss.   [*Exit.*

LORD MERLIN.

Eloped! I'd better go. If they catch me here, they'll make me *particeps criminis!* (*As he is going,* MABEL *enters at the opposite side.*)

MABEL TREVOR.

My lord—

LORD MERLIN.

Miss Trevor!

MABEL TREVOR.

Pardon this intrusion. Can your lordship grant me a few minutes private conversation?

LORD MERLIN.

As many as you please.

MABEL TREVOR.

I am anxious to—to—just now, I was quite brave in my resolution to seek this interview, but now it has come I falter and tremble.

LORD MERLIN.

Be seated. (*Hands chairs.*) Take your own time.

MABEL TREVOR.

You may judge, from my situation here, that I am friendless. It was not always thus. I had a friend once— my mother! my dear, dear mother!

LORD MERLIN.

Poor thing!—and your mother—she is dead? I see.

MABEL TREVOR.

It is not false pride makes me say that my birth was superior to the humble circumstances in which I am placed.

My mother might have—no matter! She made a foolish marriage, and her family renounced her.   The punishment was bitter for such a fault.   Widowhood followed speedily, and she was destitute.   Hopeless for herself, she struggled to live for her child.   The change was great from luxury to want—it preyed upon her sensitive frame—it killed her !

LORD MERLIN.

Come—you must not dwell on these melancholy recollections.

MABEL TREVOR.

It does me good to think of my mother—it strengthens me in all virtuous resolves—she loved me so tenderly.— The only pure love I ever knew in this selfish world.

LORD MERLIN.

And when she died, necessity forced you to accept Lady Manifold's protection ?

MABEL TREVOR.

Lady Manifold knew my mother and her history. She received me as companion to her daughter.   Companion !

LORD MERLIN.

I understand—she treats you with harshness.

MABEL TREVOR.

You cannot understand the icy coldness with which dependants are sometimes treated in a great house, as if they belonged to a lower nature, and possessed neither intelligence nor feeling—the atmosphere of stately stillness through which the poor companion creeps like a guilty creature ! That is dreadful ! She did not treat me with harshness,—she harrowed me with freezing smiles that never suffered me to forget I was a dependant. Oh !

my lord, you cannot understand that—you, basking in the
sunshine of rank and station—and how I have striven to
subdue my spirit, feeling that in my veins ran blood as
proud as theirs.

LORD MERLIN.

I understand your feelings. You desire my assistance.

MABEL TREVOR.

No—no—not that! I am coming to my purpose. But
it requires an effort—it is so strange to speak of such
things. I had the misfortune, in these unpropitious circumstances, to attract the regards of one who was born to
fortune and honours. With the heedless ardour of youth,
he seemed unconscious of the gulf that separated us. I
was not—my woman's instinct detected his love, before he
gave it utterance, and, with it, the peril of its indulgence.
He was an heir to wealth and titles—I was poor; I felt the
difference of our states, and retreated from his eloquent
gaze, which still followed me, even into solitude, where,—
I may say it now,—his name, loaded with wishes for a
worthier destiny, often mingled with my prayers!

LORD MERLIN.

Well—he avowed his love, at last? What was his fortune weighed against his happiness?

MABEL TREVOR.

I pointed out the folly, the madness of so unequal an
alliance. I appealed to his reason—his ambition; but he
saw my heart trembling through the sophistry—and—
and—I consented to become his wife.

LORD MERLIN.

With dispositions like yours, a prince might be proud of
such a wife.

MABEL TREVOR.

He had a noble kinsman upon whom all his expectations depended. That kinsman, it appeared, had other
views for his settlement in life—high connexions, aris-
tocracy, and wealth. These were the conditions of his
patronage, and disinheritance would have been the con-
sequence of our union. What should he, who stood in
this extremity, have done?

LORD MERLIN.

Kept his faith with you, like a man of honour. His integrity would have extorted respect, even from his heartless
relative.

MABEL TREVOR.

And you say this? You—I forget myself. He was
false, my lord—and baser than false.

LORD MERLIN.

He forsook you?

MABEL TREVOR.

If he had, I might have fancied a thousand excuses for
him, and wondered and hoped and died, without a reproach.
He told me that his kinsman was proud and powerful—
that he dare not fulfil his pledge. Well—it was cruel, and
my brain was crushed—but I bore it.

LORD MERLIN.

Coward!

MABEL TREVOR.

Then—he went on—he said he loved me—loved me!—
he said——I cannot—I cannot—

LORD MERLIN.

Patience—patience!

MABEL TREVOR.

Oh! God, that young affection—full of truth and joy—

should be poisoned at its very spring. He said he would
never marry—but that still, unwedded, we might—he would
have covered my whole life with infamy !

LORD MERLIN.

Villain !

MABEL TREVOR.

We parted for ever. It was my intention to leave this
house, that he might never hear of me again. But he
wrote to me, to stamp the wrong in a more deliberate
form. (*Drawing out the letter.*) There was nothing left
but to vindicate my honour. I resolved to see his proud
kinsman, and to place this letter, unopened, in his hands.

LORD MERLIN.

You were quite right.

MABEL TREVOR.

I resolved to tell him all.

LORD MERLIN.

And will do so ?

MABEL TREVOR (*rising*).

I have done so !

LORD MERLIN.

I'm paralyzed. This heartless scoundrel, then was my
nephew. Give me the letter. (*Takes the letter and puts it
up.*) I will make retributive use of it. He shall suffer
for this ! Miss Trevor, for myself I can only say that had
Mr. Sandford confided in me, you would have been spared
much misery—he irretrievable degradation. He is un-
worthy of you. Let him perish—an outcast and a beggar !

MABEL TREVOR.

Oh ! my lord, you will not cast him off?

LORD MERLIN.

I will deal with him as he deserves. The interest I felt in him is dead—it revives in you. What are your future plans? You will not refuse, at least, my counsel.

MABEL TREVOR.

I am very grateful for your goodness. I had hoped that the lapse of years might have obliterated family resentments, and that my relatives might relent.

LORD MERLIN.

Perhaps I might intercede for you—if my influence could—

MABEL TREVOR.

Possibly your lordship may have some knowledge of the Raymond family in Wiltshire?

LORD MERLIN.

Raymond?

MABEL TREVOR.

Raymond and Osterly.

LORD MERLIN.

And your mother's name was—

MABEL TREVOR.

Her name was—(*looking up*)—Your look appals me!

LORD MERLIN.

Marian—

MABEL TREVOR (*in a low, frightened tone*).

It was!

LORD MERLIN *covers his face with his hands and sinks into a chair.*

MABEL TREVOR.

My lord!

LORD MERLIN (*recovering slowly*).

The very tone of her voice—it thrilled me, and I knew not why. And Marian died of grief and suffering. Early loved and lost, her image has dwelt in my heart, and hallowed it! Marian had it been otherwise—

MABEL TREVOR.

My dear lord—

LORD MERLIN.

Her face comes back upon me through the mist of years, with all its radiant beauty, as fresh as when I first beheld it—her bright sunny smile, her clustering hair. I never saw her after her marriage. I'm glad of it; for, in my imagination, she is still the same. Memory has registered no change in that face. It beams upon me still through my gushing tears.

(MABEL, *who has gradually dropped on her knees beside him, draws a miniature from her bosom, and silently holds it before him.*)

LORD MERLIN.

Dear child!

(*He throws his arms round her with a bubbling cry, and his head sinks upon her shoulder.*)

END OF ACT IV.

ACT V.

SCENE I.

MONTAGUE's *lodgings, poorly furnished.* MONTAGUE *discovered seated at one side, and* EMILY MANIFOLD *at the other, rocking herself on a chair. Pause.*

MONTAGUE.

Well, my love, how do you feel?

EMILY MANIFOLD.

Feel? I don't feel at all.

MONTAGUE.

That's odd—I'm in a regular fever. I'm at ninety in the shade.

EMILY MANIFOLD.

We're both in the shade at present.

MONTAGUE.

Well—it's no wonder. Never was married before. 'Tis such an electrifying sensation. It sends such a rush of blood to the head.

EMILY MANIFOLD.

I'm sure it does to the cheeks. My face is burning over with shame. I shall certainly die of vexation.

MONTAGUE.

That would be very unreasonable on your wedding-day —a day destined to be celebrated in my " Life and Times."

EMILY MANIFOLD.

You shall celebrate no such thing. Just think of what you've done—of—of—of—this—this—this—it's—it's—it's —what would ma say if she could see me now !   I must have a good cry.   (*Sobs and cries hysterically.*)

MONTAGUE.

My love, you'll alarm the house—don't cry in that hilarious manner. I know how hard it is to keep down extraordinary joy—but this is a peculiar sort of house. It isn't exactly like ma's—it's a—it's a—

EMILY MANIFOLD (*with wonder and impatience*).

It's a what ?

MONTAGUE.

Why—these are lodgings, you understand—lodgings— there's somebody else overhead and another gentleman below—in short, it's not my house—I'm only a lodger—

EMILY MANIFOLD.

Overhead !—below !—and so I—I who might have been mistress of Merlin House—am married, actually married, to only a lo—lo—lodger.

MONTAGUE.

How different you are from me !   Now I could be happy with you anywhere.   I should never think of what sort of house I was in, so long as you lodged me in your heart.

EMILY.

Yes, but how would you like to lodge there, if you found somebody else overhead, and another gentleman below ? You'd like to have my whole heart to yourself, you would, without any fear of disturbing the other lo—lod—lodg— —lodgers—ers !

MONTAGUE (*aside*).

Cursed unlucky simile that.   Other lodgers in your
heart!   The thing's impossible.   I've taken it on a long
lease, and it will be too much out of repair when I've done
with it to offer any temptation to a new tenant.

EMILY MANIFOLD.

Fine speeches won't do now.   I hate 'em—I hate you—
I hate myself—I hate ma! Answer me—weren't we married
this morning?

MONTAGUE.

Incontestably.

EMILY MANIFOLD.

And this is the place you bring me home to?

MONTAGUE.

'Tis private—they'll never find us out here.

EMILY MANIFOLD.

Never—that's certain.   What do you call this odious
place?

MONTAGUE.

Central you mean.   Surrey-street.   If you put your
head out of the lobby-window, and stretch a little, you can
see the river.   Fine view of the water procession on Lord
Mayor's day!

EMILY MANIFOLD.

The very thought suffocates me.

MONTAGUE.

Don't disparage the street—Congreve the poet, lived
here.

EMILY MANIFOLD.

That shows it cannot be respectable.   Poet!   It might

do well enough for a poet—perhaps it's too good for a poet.
But for you, Montague!—for you and me!—Is this the
only room you have?

MONTAGUE.

This is my principal room.

EMILY MANIFOLD.

Is it here you receive company?

MONTAGUE.

Receive company!

EMILY MANIFOLD.

There's not a bit of decent furniture in the room.

MONTAGUE.

What do we want with furniture?

EMILY MANIFOLD.

You might as well ask me what do we want with servants,
plate, carriage, horses, or any other necessary of life!

MONTAGUE.

'Pon my life, so I might.

EMILY MANIFOLD.

Furniture!   Do you suppose my friends can sit on cane
chairs when they come to see me?   How do you think I
can live without ottomans and *fauteuils?*   Must I put two
chairs together to recline upon, and perhaps have the satisfaction of finding them break down under me?   Where are
any of the elegancies of life here?   Hangings?—mirrors?
—pictures?   I was cruelly deceived in you, Captain Montague.

MONTAGUE.

Don't call me captain—Swinford Hastings—say Swin if

you like; or Hasty—" Let us haste."—Dear Hasty—it's more like man and wife (*she turns away*). Come—come— Your wedding-day and all!—You're wrong about the furniture. Like all women, you're inconstant and inconsistent.

EMILY MANIFOLD.

How am I inconsistent?

MONTAGUE.

Remember, my angel, what you said—

> With thee content, I ask no more—
> I want not lands, nor golden store,
> Nor furnished palaces—(*furnished, observe!*)
>   —oh! Jove,
> Give me but naked walls and love!

Jove has granted your prayer—no mistake about the walls!

EMILY MANIFOLD.

That was only when you were making love to me.

MONTAGUE.

And what's to prevent me from continuing to make love to you?

EMILY MANIFOLD.

There's no occasion now. Nobody thinks of playing their cards over again, after winning the game.

MONTAGUE.

But the most experienced players like to renew the excitement by talking of their success.

EMILY MANIFOLD.

That's all very well for the winner. The loser has no pleasure in renewing the excitement. Montague, you have won me certainly—I own it—but have you won me fairly?

MONTAGUE.

If I have finessed for the odd trick, who could look in your eyes and blame me?

EMILY MANIFOLD.

Don't look so in my eyes, you wretch! And this is the odd trick is it? (*Looking round*) I'm very angry—very, very—I thought we should have made such a delightful confusion—gone off in such style—had them all in a panic —and paragraphs in the newspapers!—but this—this will kill poor ma! I'll not stay in this house another moment.

MONTAGUE.

'Pon my life, you've quite changed your character. You used to speak so low, and —

EMILY MANIFOLD.

Yes—but ma was over me then! I'm my own mistress now at any rate, and as I never had my own way with her, I'm determined I'll have it with you. Ring the bell.

MONTAGUE.

The bell?

EMILY MANIFOLD.

I insist upon it—

MONTAGUE.

But, my love—do be calm—the bell is broke—well, if you insist—(*goes to the door and returns again*). Now, you know the worst—let us calmly discuss our situation—

EMILY MANIFOLD.

No—Montague, if you love me, take me out of this house.

MONTAGUE.

If I love you !—Haven't I given up every thing for you ?
—*If*—

EMILY MANIFOLD.

You have given up ?

MONTAGUE.

To be sure I have: independence and popularity. I
used to go where I pleased, and every body was glad to
see me. It was, " Here's the Captain !"—" How very
odd ! you're the very man I was thinking of."—" There's
that dog, Montague, passing the windows without coming
in."—" Hollo ! my boy !"—" Don't forget me, my dear
fellow, at the Clarendon." Forget you? Never. That's
all over now—do you call that giving up nothing? I
was as familiar in the clubs as if I belonged to them, and
never saw any difference in the Carlton or Reform except
in the temporary ascendancy of a sauce or a fritter. My
club glories are at an end. I shall never more haunt St.
James's towards dinner-hour, with the fidelity of a post
delivery; or drop in for morning calls where there is
reason to expect evening invitations. I have given up
every thing for you.

EMILY MANIFOLD.

And what have I *not* given up for you? Liberty—the
whole rights of woman ! Flattery, conquest, tyranny, and
caprice—a house of luxury, where I was the centre of admiration—and suitors upon suitors all day long! Is that
no sacrifice ? and what has it come to ?

MONTAGUE.

'Pon my life, you do me injustice. You might have had
a worse husband. I have only one fault.

EMILY MANIFOLD.

And pray what is that?

MONTAGUE.

I'm ambitious enough to be in love with you, but so confoundedly poor as not to be indifferent to your fortune. What was I to do? I could give up the clubs—but I couldn't give up you.

EMILY MANIFOLD.

Do you really, truly love me, Montague?

MONTAGUE.

Ask the comets do they—

EMILY MANIFOLD.

That'll do. You're my husband.

MONTAGUE.

I'm proud of it.

EMILY MANIFOLD.

I won't complain any more—

MONTAGUE.

Nor I.

EMILY MANIFOLD.

On one condition.

MONTAGUE.

Name it.

EMILY MANIFOLD.

That you take me home at once to ma.

MONTAGUE.

Don't you think that's a little unreasonable so very soon after leaving her? She'd lock you up—where should I be then?

EMILY MANIFOLD.

I'd escape, and come back to you.

MONTAGUE.

You would?

EMILY MANIFOLD.

I would.

MONTAGUE.

Then I'd be the most ungrateful of husbands to put so devoted a wife to such a painful necessity. I'll compromise the difficulty. Dry up the pretty eyes, and we'll call on Lord Merlin.

EMILY MANIFOLD.

Oh! that's a good Montague.

MONTAGUE.

He's a man of sense—(*Aside*) I hope he'll ask us to dinner—and has influence with ma.

EMILY MANIFOLD.

Don't let us lose a moment.

MONTAGUE (*as they are going*).

But, my dear, (*looking round the room,*) one doesn't want the whole world to be as wise as one's self, you know— there are domestic secrets in every family.

EMILY MANIFOLD.

The very thing I was going to say to you. But you might have depended on my pride.

MONTAGUE.

I forgot that. A woman is the best confidante after all, where her husband's credit is at stake. You shall see what an heroic figure you'll make in my " Life and Times."

[*Exeunt.*

SCENE II.

Drawing-room at LORD MERLIN'S. LORD MERLIN *dis-covered seated.* BLOUNT *standing.*

LORD MERLIN.

You told Mr. Sandford I wanted to see him.

BLOUNT.

I did.

LORD MERLIN.

Then go—we must be alone.

BLOUNT.

I've business with you.

LORD MERLIN (*with vexation*).

Business!

BLOUNT.

Loop has robbed you, and run away with the money.

LORD MERLIN.

Then run after him and recover it.

BLOUNT.

Is that the way you attend to your affairs?

LORD MERLIN.

Blount, you never plagued me in this way formerly.

BLOUNT.

I had no occasion. You had only one servant then.

LORD MERLIN.

Yourself. Perhaps you are right. Crowds of lackeys,

settling like horse-flies on stairs and lobbies, are not calculated to improve one's temper.

BLOUNT.

Have you found it out at last? You're a changed man since you became a lord—changed for the worse. Master! —that's the old name I used to call you by—I never called you my lord! You'd have been ruined over and over again but for Mr. Sandford and me. We're the only true friends you have: all the rest are sycophants and plunderers.

LORD MERLIN.

Mr. Sandford?—well.

BLOUNT.

The moment he heard that Loop had decamped, he sent me after him. I found him at supper with a confederate, and recovered every farthing.

LORD MERLIN.

And pray who was his confederate?

BLOUNT.

Mistress Rose, Miss Manifold's waiting-woman. I brought them both back.

LORD MERLIN.

But Mr. Sandford—

BLOUNT.

He wouldn't let me disturb you till the business was settled. He said you were ill. That was an excuse. I know some trouble has fallen out between ye. What is it, master? Mr. Sandford loves you. I'll answer for him. You are rough to him, cross, tyrannical. I will speak: my whole life has been spent in your service faithfully, and

I have a right to speak.   You're grown unnatural to those
that love you.   I wish you were poor again.

LORD MERLIN.

An unkind wish, Blount.

BLOUNT.

The kindest! You had a heart then—what's become of it?
I see nothing of it. You used to scold me formerly for every
trifle: it did me good, and made me happy. You never
scold me now! Then, Mr. Sandford—he used to be so
merry, singing through the house, and what not!—now,
he goes about as melancholy—I can't bear to look at him.
There's something wrong—it's not my business—I beg
pardon—but Mr. Sandford loves you—don't be harsh to
him—he's young and giddy—but he loves you—don't be
harsh to him—I beg pardon, master!—don't—don't—
don't.   [*Exit.*

LORD MERLIN.

Blount's affection touches me to the core.   But he does
not know my nephew's offence. If he did, he would
condemn him as I do. Is he ashamed to meet me, that
he delays so long?—So you are come at last, Mr. Sandford.

Enter MR. SANDFORD.

SANDFORD (*aside*).

Mr. Sandford! (*to him*) Why, uncle, I—

LORD MERLIN.

No excuse.   You would have shirked this interview, if
you could.

SANDFORD.

Shirked?

LORD MERLIN.

The word belongs to the vocabulary of that town life to which you are accustomed—It implies a mean shrinking from inquiry—a cowardly evasion of responsibility. I thought you might be familiar with it.

SANDFORD.

Uncle—if you have any thing to say to me, say it at once. I cannot bear this suspense.

LORD MERLIN.

People who are indifferent to the sufferings of others, are always selfish enough to feel their own acutely. You shall hear it, sir.

SANDFORD.

Sir!—what have I done, uncle, to merit this? If you have any charge to make against me—

LORD MERLIN.

Ask your own heart, sir—I beg pardon, you have none! Look back, sir, into your recent conduct—is there nothing in it—nothing that you have reason to be ashamed of?

SANDFORD.

Many things that I regret—

LORD MERLIN.

Regret! Is there nothing that disgraces you as a gentleman and a man of honour! nothing, sir, that disentitles you for the rest of your life to any further countenance from me?

SANDFORD.

Whatever I have done, uncle, thus much I may say in my own defence, that I have done nothing contrary to

your wishes. Others may have reason to condemn me—
you at least have none.

LORD MERLIN.

I have most reason of all, sir. I find you, a youth, cast
like a waif upon the waters, without friends or means. I
draw you to the firm shore—lift you to affluence—make
you my heir—and look forward with pride and exultation
to your future course. I flatter myself I have succeeded in
forming your principles—I build all my hopes on you—all,
for I had nothing left to live for :—well, at this juncture,
with the world opening auspiciously upon you, you suddenly disappoint me, and the foolish fabric I had been
raising with so much care crumbles in a single hour into
dust !

SANDFORD.

No—no—hear me, sir—

LORD MERLIN.

That's not all. In return for my lavish kindness, you
repay me with distrust. I give your ingratitude to the
winds—let it go—but I cannot so easily dismiss your want
of confidence. Young blood may throw off benefactors in
moments of heated passion ; but there is no apology for
violating the confidence of friendship. If you thought fit
to discard the uncle, you should have remembered that he
was also the friend, and have continued to place that confidence in him which he never refused to you.

SANDFORD.

My dear uncle—but protestations are useless—I would
have confided every thing to you, without reserve, could I
have thought you would approve—

LORD MERLIN.

Approve?—approve of an act of perfidy ?

SANDFORD.

Perfidy !—no—of my attachment for Mabel. Disguise
is at an end—I see you have discovered my wretched secret,
and I am glad of it.

LORD MERLIN.

Who told you, sir, that I should disapprove of your
attachment, as you call it, for Mabel Trevor ?

SANDFORD.

Who told me ?   You did ; in words as plain as if you
named her. You said that you would have no love-matches
—that I must look for family and fortune.   I owed you
much, uncle—you had always been—(*overcome with emotion*)—at the cost of my own peace of mind, I obeyed you.

LORD MERLIN.

Obeyed me by attempting the ruin of a defenceless girl,
who had been weak enough to listen to your addresses ?

SANDFORD.

Now, indeed, I am humiliated.

LORD MERLIN.

Take care how you make me responsible for your actions.
My admonition was general—general.   It had no reference to her—I knew nothing of your design upon her.

SANDFORD.

Design ?   If ever man loved—

LORD MERLIN.

Love !   Do not profane the name.   A man who loves a
woman holds her honour as sacred as his life.   No more of
this, sir.   I desired to see you this morning, in order that
some abject expression of your remorse should be made

I

to sooth Miss Trevor's wounded feelings before we separate.

SANDFORD.

Separate ?

LORD MERLIN.

I have no wish to treat you with more severity than your
crime demands—crime, I call it crime ! nor will I add any
parting tortures to those which your own accusing
thoughts must already afflict you with.

SANDFORD.

Uncle—what would you do?

LORD MERLIN.

Upon condition that you accept a commission in a regi-
ment on foreign service, I will allow you an annuity sufficient for the simple necessities of your station.   Declining
this condition, all further intercourse ceases between us.

SANDFORD.

And you say you are not needlessly severe—oh ! uncle—
I whom you held so closely to your heart, when you shut
out all the rest of the world, and who have responded to
the pressure with a true allegiance, through all changes of
health and spirits—before, too, there were any expectations
in the case to suggest a sordid motive to my affections !

LORD MERLIN.

You would bribe my justice, boy.

SANDFORD.

No, in your justice I am safe.   For myself it is a matter
of indifference.   North, west, east, or south, it is all the
same to me now :—but wherever my destiny casts me, my

anxiety for her will only be increased by time and distance.

LORD MERLIN.

It will be a waste of sympathy which might be more wisely employed. Miss Trevor leaves London to-morrow, and from that moment your fortunes are flung as widely asunder as if you dwelt apart in the extremities of the earth. (*Enter* TOM *with a card which he hands to* LORD MERLIN.) A provoking interruption—tell them I'm engaged—show them into the next room.

Enter CAPTAIN MONTAGUE *and* EMILY.

[*Exit* TOM.

MONTAGUE.

It's no use—take no refusals—no time for saying no—is it, my dear? You see, my lord, I'm as good as my word—ran away with her this morning.

LORD MERLIN.

Your expedition, Captain, takes me by surprise. I scarcely looked for the honour of a visit so early.

MONTAGUE.

True—out of course—but extreme cases, you know, require extreme measures. The fact is—

LORD MERLIN.

Excuse me. (*To* SANDFORD) You had better retire to your room, till I get rid of these troublesome visiters. I'll send for you when I'm alone. (*Exit* SANDFORD.) And you are actually married?

MONTAGUE.

Actually—in my own parish—strictly private—no parade —no bell-ringers—no nonsense—over in ten minutes—but

I 2

my wife had some little scruples about—hem !—her ma !
and knowing your lordship's eminent good-nature, would
have me just call upon you to ask your interference—

EMILY MANIFOLD.

I hope your lordship isn't angry with me for giving the
preference to the Captain !

LORD MERLIN.

Why should I be angry to see you so happy ?   Have
you been home yet ?

EMILY MANIFOLD.

Home ?

MONTAGUE.

Home ? oh ! yes—no—you mean—

LORD MERLIN.

Of course you've taken her to your own house, her
future home ?

MONTAGUE.

My house ?—eh !—oh !—certainly—she's quite charmed
—eh ! my love ?—so different, you know, to be mistress
of her own establishment—

EMILY MANIFOLD.

Very different—I'm quite charmed !

LORD MERLIN (*half aside to* MONTAGUE).

You don't intend to lay her up half the year—like a
ship in ordinary !

MONTAGUE.

I hope, with ma's help, to set her afloat, by and by, like
a ship in full sail !

Enter TOM *with another card.*

LORD MERLIN.

This is very awkward.   What am I to do with you?

MONTAGUE.

With us? what's the matter?

LORD MERLIN.

Lady Manifold and Sir Gregory are coming up.

MONTAGUE.

Oh! my lord, hide us anywhere—striking incident this for my " Life and Times."

EMILY MANIFOLD.

I shall faint—I wouldn't see ma to-day for—oh! where shall we go?

LORD MERLIN.

Into this apartment, if you will have patience to remain till I release you.

EMILY MANIFOLD.

Thank you, my lord—

MONTAGUE.

Under the table, if necessary.

[*Exeunt into the inner room.*

(TOM *showing in* LADY MANIFOLD *and* SIR GREGORY PLUMP, *and goes off.*)

LADY MANIFOLD.

Oh! my lord—the dreadful intelligence I have to communicate—I know you'll be shocked—judge of my horror and mortification—that wretch Montague—the pitiful, beggarly reptile, that lives, no one knows how and where, has taken advantage of the confiding simplicity of my poor child, and inveigled her away—perhaps, at this moment, she's hiding her grief in some miserable garret. (*During the above* MONTAGUE *and* EMILY MANIFOLD *occasionally peep out.*)

LORD MERLIN.

I hope not so bad. The care with which you educated her—

LADY MANIFOLD.

I've nothing to reproach myself with on that score, certainly.

LORD MERLIN.

The excellent example you showed her—

LADY MANIFOLD.

True—true—

LORD MERLIN.

The pains you took to provide a husband for her—suitable to her years—

LADY MANIFOLD.

Y—e—s! y—e—s!

LORD MERLIN.

It is surely not possible so much maternal tenderness and such judicious counsels should be so ill repaid.

LADY MANIFOLD.

One would think not.

LORD MERLIN.

Now had you filled her head with folly and pride—

LADY MANIFOLD.

Ah!

LORD MERLIN.

Had you nursed her vanity, excluded every useful accomplishment and made her egregiously frivolous and artificial—

LADY MANIFOLD.

Ah !—if—I—had—

LORD MERLIN.

Why, if you had, nobody could wonder that she should deceive you, and throw herself away upon just such a beggarly reptile as you've described. But is the matter really gone so far as you imagine ?

LADY MANIFOLD.

But I tell you, my lord, it has—Montague has entrapped her into it.

LORD MERLIN.

Suppose it was with her own consent ?

LADY MANIFOLD.

If I thought her capable of such an act—I'd—

LORD MERLIN.

Don't pronounce a rash sentence. You'd remember that, after all, she was but a foolish girl, and you'd call to mind that when you were young and giddy, like her, you made a runaway match yourself ! (*During this speech* LORD MERLIN *makes signs to* MONTAGUE *and* EMILY, *who come down the stage and kneel.*) The culprits are at your feet, madam. (*Moving aside and discovering them.*)

SIR GREGORY PLUMP.

And you will forgive them.

LADY MANIFOLD.

In one word, are you married ?

EMILY MANIFOLD.

Yes—ma.

MONTAGUE.

Allow me to present Mrs. Montague!

LADY MANIFOLD.

It's a conspiracy. You're all in a conspiracy. Don't come near me—serpent ! Sir Gregory, you're an accessory.—

SIR GREGORY PLUMP.

After the fact, your ladyship.

LADY MANIFOLD.

And you, my lord, I understand your sneers. I filled her head with vanity—I showed her an excellent example —I made a runaway match, but it was with a baronet, let me tell you—a member of parliament—a gentleman, who settled a jointure on me, and who brought me home to a splendid mansion, not a starving stroller who has neither house nor home. As for you, Miss Manifold, *alias* Mrs. —pah !—you were always a cunning, scheming little thing ; but you've made your bed, and a pretty bed it is. I'll— I'll—get me some water—never—I'll never—

SIR GREGORY PLUMP.

You agitate yourself.

LADY MANIFOLD.

Don't speak to me !

EMILY MANIFOLD.

You know, ma, you encouraged me to flirt with the captain.

MONTAGUE.

And, 'pon my life, your ladyship's commands placed me in so delicate a predicament that—

LADY MANIFOLD.

I wonder they don't say I connived at it! Their depravity overwhelms me. Had there been a fortune in the case (MONTAGUE *looks blank*), or interest even to get the fellow in full pay, or any one solid recommendation at either side ; but a poor rat that can hardly keep soul and body together, to marry a girl without a penny, depravity !

MONTAGUE.

But, surely—

EMILY MANIFOLD.

But, dear ma, you know I am your daughter after all.

LADY MANIFOLD.

There—there—no tears—you know, Emily, all I've done for you—you know I loved you—I—I—there—there—get up, child—I—my own poor Emily !—(*throws her arms round her neck*)—but remember, I haven't forgiven you for all that!

LORD MERLIN.

Hadn't we better leave them to reflect on their enormities ? You can't inflict a greater punishment on them than to leave them together. (*Drawing her towards the side.*) Sir Gregory, give her ladyship your arm.

LADY MANIFOLD.

It's pleasant to have a friend in one's trouble. Ah ! Sir Gregory !

SIR GREGORY PLUMP.

So it is.

LADY MANIFOLD.

I don't see why I should imbitter my whole life fretting about her.

SIR GREGORY PLUMP.

Nor I, neither.

LADY MANIFOLD.

Besides, Sir Richard left me sole control over my little property during my life, and they deserve to suffer.

LORD MERLIN.

Depend upon it, the turtle-doves are as miserable as your ladyship can desire!

[*Exeunt* LADY MANIFOLD, LORD MERLIN, and SIR GREGORY PLUMP.

(CAPTAIN MONTAGUE *and* EMILY *exchange looks of embarrassment—an awkward pause.*)

MONTAGUE.

Wife!

EMILY MANIFOLD.

Husband!

MONTAGUE.

I thought, my dear, you had a fortune—something under a plum!

EMILY MANIFOLD.

I thought, my dear, you married me for love!

MONTAGUE.

Well—so I did—but a little settlement—

EMILY MANIFOLD.

I settled myself upon you.

MONTAGUE.

I forgot that.

EMILY MANIFOLD.

Some settlements may be revoked—

MONTAGUE.

So they may.

EMILY MANIFOLD.

Mine cannot.

MONTAGUE.

No—damn it!—it's for life!

Enter LORD MERLIN.

LORD MERLIN.

Go to her—go to her. Sir Gregory is pleading for you
with the resolution of a martyr. Every argument will cost
him a thousand pounds. Watch your opportunity, and ply
her with penitence. No words—go! (*Exeunt* CAPTAIN
MONTAGUE *and* EMILY.) Well—I've disposed of them
at last; and now to bring to issue the business that lies
heaviest upon my heart. (*He goes out, and in a few moments
returns, leading in* MABEL.) I have seen my nephew, Miss
Trevor, and communicated to him my final resolution. I
have also apprized him of your approaching departure from
London ; and now nothing remains but that he ask pardon,
before he takes leave of England.

MABEL TREVOR.

Indeed, my lord, I do not require it. I am satisfied—

LORD MERLIN.

Young lady,—*I* am not. (*Rings the bell.*) He goes
into another country, amongst strangers—(*Enter* TOM)—
Tell Mr. Sandford to come here—(*Exit* TOM)—he must
take a solemn lesson with him. Imperfect atonement
would give impunity to future errors.

MABEL TREVOR (*agitated*).

Do not press this upon me. Suffer me to withdraw.

LORD MERLIN.

Then you repent your resolution?

MABEL TREVOR.

Oh! no, my lord—my resolution is taken. Only do not
ask me to witness his humiliation.

LORD MERLIN.

Humiliation! It will be useful to him, and it is due to
you. Be true to yourself. He is here.

Enter SANDFORD.

SANDFORD.

Mabel!

(LORD MERLIN *remains silent, observing them.*)

MABEL (*after a violent effort, which she finally overcomes.*)

My lord—

LORD MERLIN (*to* SANDFORD).

I will not oppress you with any needless reference to the past. At my request, Miss Trevor is here to receive, in my presence, such an apology for your conduct as your own sense of its unworthiness may suggest.

SANDFORD (*aside*).

If I could lift my eyes to hers—

LORD MERLIN.

Well—you are silent?

SANDFORD.

My lord, I cannot find words—

LORD MERLIN.

Oh! You are at a loss for words—you were not at a loss for words when you contemplated the commission of a flagrant wrong.

SANDFORD.

Spare me, and I will try to speak.

LORD MERLIN.

Bear this in mind—your contrition—I hope it is sincere! —can have no influence on my determination. Do not deceive yourself upon that point. Whatever you say, must be voluntary.

SANDFORD.

My lord, you bear hardly upon me; but I acknowledge the rigorous justice with which you treat me. If I cannot speak freely, it is shame alone that checks me. Miss Trevor, could I draw out my heart before you that you might see its secret emotions, there would be no need to tell you what I have suffered, and what I am suffering now. I dare not ask your pardon—he who, possessing your love, could have abused it even in thought, does not deserve pardon. But my brain was distracted at that fatal interview—I had but one fear before me,—the fear of losing you—I spoke incoherently like one in a frenzy—I believed my uncle would never consent to our union—oh! if I had had the courage to consult him! But it is too late now—my guilt was unpremeditated, and it was scarcely uttered when my soul was filled with the bitterness of remorse.

MABEL TREVOR.

No more—I entreat, no more!

LORD MERLIN.

You say it was unpremeditated?

SANDFORD.

So unpremeditated, that I can hardly gather up a clear recollection of what happened. I remember nothing but that in a moment of impetuous passion I forfeited that confidence to the sacred maintenance of which I looked for a life of honour and happiness.

LORD MERLIN.

It was rather a protracted moment, since it lasted till the next day, when you deliberately confirmed the insult by writing to Miss Trevor. Oh! Sandford, Sandford, this flimsy excuse only makes the matter worse.

SANDFORD.

I did write to her—can you produce my letter?

LORD MERLIN.

I can, to your confusion—(taking it out)—Miss Trevor

handed it to me as she received it, and I have preserved
it unopened—do not force me to read it.

SANDFORD.

Then you have not read it ?   Give it to me—

LORD MERLIN.

Why are you so eager to repossess it ?

SANDFORD.

Only to place it in her hands again.

LORD MERLIN.

You wilfully draw down the consequences. Nothing—
nothing but your own folly could have induced me to
expose you any further—(*breaks the seal, and reads*). " I
tremble with agitation while I write. Hardly conscious of
what I said to you yesterday, but too well assured of the
wound I inflicted on your feelings, I hasten to make all
the atonement in my power. I relinquish for ever all
expectations from my uncle. Even my uncle himself, when
he knows all, will pardon me; but were the sacrifice, if it
be a sacrifice, a thousand times greater than it is, I would
make it cheerfully. On my knees, I entreat for pardon. Do
not destroy one who loves you with so true a faith."

SANDFORD (*throwing himself on his knees before* MABEL).

And again upon my knees, I sue for pardon—and here,
in my uncle's presence, again I relinquish all dreams of
rank and wealth, if you will pity and forgive me !

MABEL TREVOR.

Forgive !—my eyes are dim with tears !

LORD MERLIN.

Raise him from the ground. It is no time for talking.
Bob, I have done you injustice, but it was your own fault.

This little trial of your principles will make you value each other the more. (*He joins their hands.*) Be happy—be happy! You relinquish all dreams of wealth, Bob!—I take you at your word—it shall be no dream, but a reality.

Enter LADY MANIFOLD *and* SIR GREGORY, *followed by* CAPTAIN MONTAGUE *and* EMILY.

LADY MANIFOLD.

Well—well. Sir Gregory and I will consider of it. You can't expect that I should cut down my own expenditure to put a premium upon your disobedience; no, that's rather too much.

SIR GREGORY PLUMP.

It would be highly unreasonable. (*To* EMILY) How could you expect your mother to do any thing of the kind? (*To* LADY MANIFOLD) But, as you mentioned, there's room enough for them in the house, and, when a certain event takes place, you know we will spend a few months at Plump Park, and they can keep the establishment in town in order for us; and, by and by, who knows but—

LADY MANIFOLD.

Ah! Sir Gregory, your heart runs before your head; and if there were as many mortgages on Plump Park as there are upon your benevolence, I'm afraid the establishment in town would be the only resource for us all. However, I forgive them.

EMILY MANIFOLD.

Oh! ma, then you'll take me home to-day?

MONTAGUE.

You see, your ladyship, although I ran away with your daughter, I didn't attempt to alienate her domestic affections.

LORD MERLIN (*coming forward*).

So I find you have agreed upon a truce. I thought

you would. And if I don't mistake, Gregory, I detect in
her ladyship's bashful glances the tremulous indications
of a surrender. She has got a nibble at last. What a
festival of weddings we shall have! I am the only solitary amongst ye—no, not solitary. Here (SANDFORD *and*
MABEL *come forward*) is my bridal. In them I revive,
and they will crown my closing years with grateful love.

LADY MANIFOLD.

Mabel—Mr. Sandford. What does this mean?

LORD MERLIN.

I had forgotten. Allow me to introduce Mabel Trevor
—linked to my heart by old and tender memories—as the
betrothed of my nephew. While you have been arranging
your wedding diplomacies in the next room, we have been
settling similar preliminaries here.

LADY MANIFOLD (*half aside*).

Is it possible? Well—I'll put the best face I can upon
it. (*Crossing over to* MABEL) My dear Mabel, suffer
me to wish you joy. I am really quite enchanted at this
delightful turn of fortune. Mr. Sandford, I sincerely con-
gratulate you. You've got a treasure in her.

LORD MERLIN (*half aside*).

What a wonderful forcing-bed is prosperity for the
growth of sudden friendships! (*To* SANDFORD) You
hear what her ladyship says, Bob—you have got a treasure
in her. Let that truth sink into your heart, and regulate
your life. Guard your treasure well—it is more precious
than gold. When the pomp of heraldry perishes in
desolate vanities round its possessor, the pure affection of
woman survives to him, superior in its fidelity to all the
shows of fortune, or the accidents of birth.

THE END.

www.ingramcontent.com/pod-product-compliance
Lightning Source LLC
Chambersburg PA
CBHW031120020726
47495CB00007B/2277